Praise for *Nauetakuan, a silence for a noise*

"A love letter to residential school survivors, dedicated to their descendants... To create the universe of *Nauetakuan, a silence for a noise*, populated by giant animals and marvelous creatures, including the thunderbird, Natasha Kanapé Fontaine was inspired by her own dreams, various native myths, and ancient legends taught to her by Joséphine Bacon." —*Le Devoir*

"Poet, singer, actress, and Innu activist, the talented Natasha Kanapé Fontaine has written a hard-hitting first novel, which cuts through us like a lightning bolt." —*Le Journal de Montréal*

Nauetakuan,
a silence for a noise

Natasha Kanapé Fontaine
TRANSLATED BY HOWARD SCOTT

LITERATURE IN TRANSLATION SERIES

Book*hug Press
Toronto 2024

FIRST ENGLISH EDITION
First published as *Nauetakuan, un silence un bruit* by Natasha Kanapé
Fontaine
Original text © 2021 by Les Éditions XYZ inc.
English translation © 2024 by Howard Scott

Library and Archives Canada Cataloguing in Publication

Title: Nauetakaun, a silence for a noise / Natasha Kanapé Fontaine ;
translated by Howard Scott.
Other titles: Nauetakuan, un silence pour un bruit. English
Names: Kanapé Fontaine, Natasha, 1991- author. | Scott, Howard,
1952- translator.
Description: Translation of: Nauetakuan, un silence pour un bruit. |
Includes bibliographical references and index.
Identifiers: Canadiana (print) 202305711X | Canadiana (ebook)
20230571174
   ISBN 9781771668941 (softcover)
   ISBN 9781771668989 (EPUB)
Classification: LCC PS8621.A49 N3813 2024 | DDC C843/.6—dc23

The production of this book was made possible through the gener-
ous assistance of the Canada Council for the Arts and the Ontario
Arts Council. Book*hug Press also acknowledges the support of the
Government of Canada through the Canada Book Fund and the
Government of Ontario through the Ontario Book Publishing Tax
Credit and the Ontario Book Fund.

 Canada Council Conseil des Arts
for the Arts du Canada

Book*hug Press acknowledges that the land on which we operate is
the traditional territory of many nations, including the Mississaugas
of the Credit, the Anishnabeg, the Chippewa, the Haudenosaunee,
and the Wendat peoples. We recognize the enduring presence of many
diverse First Nations, Inuit, and Métis peoples, and are grateful for the
opportunity to meet, work, and learn on this territory.

for Andrew
for Suzanna

Nauetakuan (ńauetakuan): the noise is heard very far away.
Pessamit pronunciation: [laːweːtaːkwən]

Innu Dictionary,
https://dictionary.innu-aimun.ca/Words

Lives go by. People's names, the words of lovers, children's cries, screams of fear, the roar of engines. Cars stream past. Everywhere in the streets of Montreal, everywhere in other cities, the alleys, the country roads, in Nitassinan. Speeding trains, fingers on computer keyboards. Paddle strokes on winding rivers. Everywhere on the planet. Thousands of satellites, with all their static. Every second is filled with their vibrations.

Above our heads, airplanes fly to distant destinations. Sometimes we can make out the symbols of the countries they come from. They're so far above us, and yet I can recognize the drone of the different engines even from inside my apartment.

Down on the ground, every day, Pie-IX Boulevard fills up during rush hour. Waves and swells of cars. Last week, the neighbours on our left cut down several trees in the yard. Some of those still standing have already lost their leaves.

Sometimes I want to shut myself up in this apartment and just soak up the shadows. The sound of the fridge has filled our home for a long time. No one hears it anymore. I confuse it with silence. But everything that's happening outside, all around, seeps in. Inhabits our bodies. The soundtrack of a life we're trying to fill.

All of life is filled with itself, and yet human beings have the ability to ignore it. To hide from its meaning. Is it a perceptual disorder? Like a vision problem maybe. A sensitivity disorder? Like not knowing how to feel that another being is sharing the same room with you, the same time in the present. It's the cat.

Behind all of it, a dull sound persists, eluding awareness. They say Earth vibrates at 7.8 hertz, which changes according to natural phenomena like lightning. It can be neither named nor touched. How can you interpret a thing that is perceived but not seen? An ancient fir tree that falls in the middle of a forest during a fire.

These are the thoughts I'm having—about me, about my life now, that it's an empty shell. There's nothing that makes my heart beat faster, nothing that excites me. Everything has a noise inside.

And every day, on the street, cars honk, trucks growl, semis rumble like the storms of August, and even the children in strollers on the sidewalks are screaming for more.

The applause rings out, creating a festive feeling throughout the main hall of the Musée d'art contemporain.
Shouting above the din, the curator invites guests to
help themselves to some hors d'oeuvres to conclude
the opening of the exhibition. Monica heads toward
the food table, just ahead of other hungry patrons who
are heading in the same direction. After grabbing some
grapes and cheese cubes, she slips behind the mob now
swarming around the trays and walks over to grab a
glass of wine before moving away. She weaves slowly
through the crowd, taking her first sips, then she stops
and looks up at a work of art at the far end of the room,
a little above the throng of enthusiastic visitors standing
in front of it. The photograph is of a woman lying on
her side, her back to the lens. Her black hair is streaked
with platinum, a white sheet covers her hips, and there
is a huge scar across her back, stitched with a row of red
glass beads. There are also a few white threads that look
like stitches. The whole image is both troubling and
captivating.

Monica goes closer, walking around the small group
of guests. Seconds tick by and her eyes scrutinize the
woman's back. She's lying on a surface that looks like an
immaculate hospital bed, but without metal bars. *Fringe.*

That's the title of the piece, a large photograph mounted in a light box. Monica feels something stir in her chest. It's not the time for her. It's too subtle to be analyzed. She tries to deny what she feels deep inside. Within her disordered thoughts, she tries to draw an uncertain parallel between those strings of red beads and her own life.

Strings like lines encircling the globe of the Earth. If only there were a direction to their trajectory, if only gravity were not the only force giving them movement.

Monica walks over to another piece by the Anishinaabe artist featured in the exhibition. All her work deals with the injustices experienced by First Peoples in Canada. Rebecca Belmore: that's the name on the labels for each installation, painting, and photograph...

Monica is still finding all this out at the retrospective's opening. Until now, she barely knew Belmore's name. Earlier that week, her colleagues at the Université du Québec à Montréal student newspaper suggested she cover the opening of the exhibition, which the museum seemed so proud to promote. Monica said yes without giving it much thought, because she wanted to see the original works, she told herself, instead of just scrolling through photos and bland criticism on her computer screen without getting a real feel for the effect.

The installation in front of her is gripping, instantly. On the floor, what looks like a teenager wearing a hoodie seen from behind, their head covered. Black hair tumbles out from under fabric, fanning out in all directions, and as far as Monica's feet. It hits her.

Monica moves on to another installation. This time, she stops in front of two big white facing walls on which two videos are simultaneously projected. A brown-skinned woman with dishevelled black hair, wearing only a red coat made of light fabric that's too thin for the forest, the snow, and the cold, is running, out of breath, on a path that's barely visible in the white winter. A man follows her, apparently as panicked and desperate as she is. Monica contemplates the work for a moment, identifying with the lost woman. Both projections depict the same scene, with one small difference: one seems to be an external point of view, showing the couple's perspective, while the other sees the action through the eyes of their pursuers. Monica steps forward to read the label.

March 5, 1819 (2008). Demasduit, a Beothuk young woman, is captured by English settlers at Red Indian Lake. Her husband, Nonosabasut, dies trying to protect her.

A shiver raises the hair on Monica's arms.

How can anyone understand, at the moment it occurs, the first feelings of injustice that dare crawl under your skin? How can you avert the effects of that injustice entering your consciousness, the emotions it precedes and the emotions it follows, and that sometimes even lead to the meandering paths of memory?

Even born warriors have no armour at birth. The armour must be fashioned in the course of encounters, discoveries. Ideally, there would be some decently resistant material to use for protection as soon as the first challenges arise, a custom-made helmet, impenetrable protection.

Monica continues to walk through the exhibition, deeply moved, spellbound, thoughtful, silent. And suddenly it hits her. It doesn't change anything. But no one has spoken to her since she got there.

Who would anyway? Who knows her? *I'm an ordinary girl.* What would she have to say in the ambient noise, the fleeting conversations, the self-conscious laughter? *I'm not like these people.*

She forgets why she's in the museum today, why she came to the event. She's no longer there just for herself. It all speaks to her, it is all disturbing. An invisible shadow wraps around her, numbing her.

She ends up in a small black room, in front of a giant screen, around which a string of light bulbs glows with a reassuring orange-yellow light. A video is beginning. In this performance, Rebecca Belmore appears in an alley. The camera rotates briefly around her, revealing a small group of people off to one side, their arms close to their bodies. They are wearing sunglasses and sometimes they smile.

Belmore is sombre, serious, and she walks in a long red dress, looking down at the asphalt.

In her hand, she holds a heavy hammer.

She steps forward and stands in front of a utility pole near a tall grey fence.

She takes a big nail from a bucket and grabs a part of her dress. She nails the dress to the post, hammering hard.

Then she yanks her dress violently, as if to free herself from the sudden bond.

She repeats the gesture. Twice, three times, four. Each time, her dress tears, and scraps of fabric fall to the ground.

She continues for several minutes. She keeps going until there's nothing left but the sleeves, torn at the edges. Underneath, she wears white clothes, a soft tank top, panties. The contrast makes her dark skin look darker.

Her red dress, in tatters, lies at the foot of the post, which is riddled with nails.

Monica sits motionless on a little wooden bench in the dark room. Her tears flow of their own accord, without stopping. There are no sobs, no shuddering, only silence. Why is she crying? She tries to hold it all in. What's the warmth deep in her belly, the sudden whirlwind in her chest? What's with the tears?

Belmore opens a bag and pulls out a pair of jeans, which she puts on. On the ground are pails containing flowers. She solemnly takes a bunch of red roses and turns to the audience, who are still watching her in silence.

On her arms, several names are written in black Sharpie. A rose is clamped between her teeth, and she slides the flower from the stem end to remove the leaves and petals, which she spits out.

She shouts a name: *CINDYYYY!*

Cindy. Her voice bounces off the buildings, echoing through the empty spaces between them. Repeating the same gesture, she shouts other names: *Sarah, Mandy, Christine...* The names of women. Women never found. Murdered, disappeared. Missing women. The litany is piercing and charged with emotion, etched with the hope of bringing back their absent bodies. After the recitation, in the strange calm of the city, comes the coup de grâce: a child, in the far distance, on a balcony or in another alley, starts to cry. The unexpected weeping rings out like a soul looking for the way home. The effect is gripping, terrifying. Every person in the audience feels a shiver run up their spine.

Monica is weeping.

She opens her hands, which rest on her knees. For a

moment she considers the mascara streaks between the lines of her palms. That inert design, a trajectory deviating from its initial course.

A young woman comes into the small projection room. She walks softly, respecting the silence in the room, and sits down on the same bench, on Monica's left. The colour of the lights and of Rebecca's dress bathe her brown face in a warm glow. She watches the flickering screen for a moment. Monica shifts, and the woman, distracted, turns to her, noticing her open hands.

"Are you okay?"

Monica looks at the young woman with surprise, a little ashamed. Usually, she doesn't cry in public. Her eyes are still full of tears, her cheeks wet. It takes her an instant to read the features of the woman who pulled her from her ruminations—the high cheekbones, the smooth black hair shining in the darkness. They seem about the same age. The stranger is holding a purple jersey decorated with colourful birds.

"Yes, I'm okay." Monica sniffles and tries to hide her face with the back of her hand.

The young woman hands her her jersey, letting her know it's okay, she can use it to wipe her tears. "Here. I understand."

Both look up at the work that has been playing on a loop since the beginning of the exhibition, and for even longer before.

"That one really gets to me too," the woman goes on.

Monica contemplates the stranger's attentive eyes before turning back to the giant video screen. "Is it true?"

"Is what true?"

"That there are so many who go missing—Indigenous women?"

"There are places where it's much worse. Out west, in BC, there's a road people call the Highway of Tears..." She goes quiet. Her voice breaks. "It's the only road that goes from the big cities to the north... They call it that because there's nothing for kilometres, not even cops. It's well-known that Indigenous women vanish without a trace up there."

The two women watch the Rebecca Belmore performance piece for a little while longer. The video loops back again to the scene of the artist tearing off rose leaves and petals with her lips and her teeth.

"My name's Katherine."

"Nice to meet you. I'm Monica."

"Where are you from?"

"Well...I live here, in Montreal."

"I mean your people. What community are you from?"

"Oh. My mother raised me in Forestville, but we're from Pessamit."

"Oh, yeah! I'm from Kitigan Zibi."

"Kitigan Zibi?"

"Near Maniwaki, so close it's almost the same thing. When you say you're going to Maniwaki, that can mean you're going to Kitigan Zibi!" Katherine laughs. "Especially since people in the city have never heard of it."

"Yeah, I've never heard the name. I'm not even sure if I know where Maniwaki is."

"It's like three and a half hours from Montreal. It's really not far. Pessamit is about a nine-hour drive, I think, right? Ha ha! Now, that's far!"

"Yeah, it's really far. Well, Forestville too; it's the same thing. It's half an hour from there."

"In a way I'm from up there too, because my grandfather was Innu. He went to live in Kitigan Zibi when he was pretty young, to marry my grandmother. I have his name, St-Onge. But I changed it to Shetush, since that's more Innu. And Anishinaabe too, of course, ha ha!"

"Hey! That's cool. I'm just Hervieux. I can't very well change that into Innu, can I? I don't even know how it would sound," Monica says with a laugh.

"Ha ha ha! But do you speak Innu-aimun?"

"No, but I did speak it when I was little, except after that I kind of lost it. My mother pretty much raised me alone, in a town where there were almost only Québécois, not many Innus, so… And we didn't go to the village that often. Anyway. I don't speak it much anymore." Monica again punctuates her words with a laugh that sounds a little sad. "It doesn't matter. You know, I'm supposed to speak Anishinaabe too, but I don't speak it much anymore. I don't have enough people to talk to. With time, you know, I speak it less and less, and it really feels like I'm losing words. I speak French because I learned it by hearing it, but other than that, in school, everything was in English."

Monica smiles at Katherine and turns back to the video. At the end of another complete loop, she stands up. "Anyway…it's Katherine, right? Did you just get here? Do you want to go see something else? I was almost done with my visit."

"Yeah, I've been here awhile. And I've already seen the exhibition too. I saw it in Toronto, when it opened. Last year, I think it was. But I wanted to see it again… Rebecca is huge in contemporary art. It's kind of ironic that she's represented Canada several times internation-ally. Anyway…"

Other people are filing into the small space to watch

the video as well, so the two young women give up their bench and go back to the main room. Monica realizes she's still holding Katherine's balled-up purple jersey against her belly and hands it back, smoothing it out as best she can.

"Wow, that's crazy! I didn't know her before. It's really something what she's doing."

"Yeah, it's deep. It really gets to me. I've always followed her work. She's really loud and clear about what the world is going through very quietly. Not necessarily with words, but with art. She's my role model, I'd say."

"Are you an artist?"

"Not really. I bead, I make earrings, but that's about it." Katherine chuckles.

"Ha ha ha! You *are* an artist! You create earrings, that's pretty cool."

"Yeah, it's mostly just to pass the time, it makes me feel good. I'm in school for sociology. But I do sell some, sometimes, my beadwork." Katherine smiles.

"Really? I'd love to order a pair sometime, for the next time I have a date! Actually, I'm supposed to be writing an article for my university newspaper. Would you have time to chat a bit more about the exhibition? I kind of think…I think you could explain things to me that maybe I don't quite get."

"Sure! Come on, we can head out and get a coffee downstairs if you want," Katherine says, as they head toward the exit.

At the counter in the Van Houtte, they each order a large latte and keep talking, their conversation easy and full of laughter. Monica tells Katherine that she's studying art history. She was in her fourth semester but dropped out of most of her classes. She's always been interested in art in general, but she has a hard time articulating her thoughts on contemporary art, on what galleries are showing currently. What excites her is Gaudí's architecture in Spain, abstract paintings in museums, Frida Kahlo's murals in Mexico City—all of Kahlo's work, in fact, definitely—and lots of other things she's curious about, wherever they are. In the beginning, she was mostly involved in the little UQAM student newspaper, *Sans détours*, because she was looking for a way to get to visit more monuments and art exhibitions, to absorb and analyze what's being created all over the place.

When their drinks are up, the two young women grab them and head toward the Place des Arts exit to walk along Sainte-Catherine Street, trading personal anecdotes and comments about the exhibit.

Monica wants to know more about where Katherine was born, where she comes from. Katherine is very close to her mother and talks a lot about her. She grew up between Kitigan Zibi and Toronto. When Monica tells her she knows just about as little about Toronto as she does about Kitigan Zibi, aside from being able to recognize the CN Tower in a photo, Katherine laughs excitedly. The big city by the water has always been a meeting place of the Anishinaabe, Ojibway, Cree, Wendat, and Haudenosaunee, she tells her, an important meeting place among the Nations, like Tio'tia:ke/Montreal. It's because the Great Lakes have long been a major travel route, she explains. When you're Indigenous, and from one of those Nations, there's something so familiar about that sublime stretch of land, with the Great Lakes as its beating heart.

Monica's eyes grow wider, and Katherine bursts out laughing. She didn't always know all that either, she confesses. Three years ago, because she wanted to know what her mother went through before having kids, she followed in her footsteps and went to study anthropology for a year at York University, in the big city of Tkaronto. It was more an excuse than about getting a degree, and she came back to Tio'tia:ke/Montreal at the end of the year, though not without having learned a thing or two. In the meantime, her parents had moved to Longueuil. Her mother works with the group Quebec Native Women, in Kahnawake, and her father works downtown for a legal firm.

"They're pretty settled and quiet now, but my mother travelled quite a bit in her day. Like, for instance, she knows about ceremonies, and she still goes to sun dances every year, especially in Arizona, with the Navajo, but also all over the continent, and in Québec. She keeps encouraging me to ramble a bit while I'm in school... *Enjoy yourself while you can, girl!*"

Monica listens attentively to Katherine's open, light-hearted chatter. Her new friend likes to laugh, and she sees herself in that. Since coming to Montreal, she hasn't really found anyone who wants to laugh as much as she does. When Katherine starts talking about ceremonies, she feels something jab her arm.

"Ouch!"

"What?"

"I don't know, maybe scratched myself on something. Like something pinched me."

"Maybe you got stung by a bee? There're always some around the Place des Arts gardens, up there."

"I don't know..."

Katherine looks at her for a second.

"What?"

"Do you know the ceremonies, Monica?"

"No, why?"

"Just asking. When we talk about spirits, something interesting always happens. Come to think of it, I didn't really see any bees around."

"Huh? Is something happening, sort of?"

"Like, you got pinched by…nothing."

"Okay. Um, is that supposed to mean something?"

"I'll tell you later!" Katherine bursts into laughter and skips toward the stairs to the Maison symphonique concert hall.

"Come on! No, tell me now! Why do you want to wait until later?"

"Because that's the way it iiiiis!" Katherine dances up the stairs.

"Katherine!"

"What? Stop thinking about it! Come on, I'll put on some music!" Katherine holds her latte in one hand and her phone in the other, trying to thumb the screen to start playing a song. "I always have this tune in my head. I'll put it on!"

Monica hears the first notes of "Jerusalema," by Master KG, featuring the South African singer Nomcebo Zikode. Katherine turns up the volume and starts darting her feet back and forth on the ground.

"Katherine, you're crazy, everybody's looking at us!"

"Come on, let's go, I'm sure you love dancing too!"

Monica joins Katherine on the paved area at the top of the stairs. From there, they can see people going by on the pedestrian street.

"I saw this move on TikTok—check it out!" Katherine

tries to recreate the choreography of the Jerusalema challenge.

Monica joins in, imitating her, but has to stop, she's too out of breath. "Ha ha, I can't keep up with you!"

Soon Katherine is panting too, and they both collapse on the ground, exhausted and laughing. After catching her breath, Katherine explains that the song, in Zulu, is a prayer for protection addressed to God, or whatever great power you believe in, with good dancing vibes.

Inspired, Monica gets up and starts to dance again, her heart pounding to the rhythm of the intoxicating music. And the whole world slows down. Katherine joins the dance, and they make up their own choreography, their own challenge. Smiling, Monica looks up, toward the blue sky over Montreal. People walk by and smile at them.

Monica hears a dull noise behind her and turns her head, looking for its source. She keeps dancing, but her initial enthusiasm is gone. Is it her ears that are inventing that strange whistling sound? She turns to Katherine, who stops dancing too and comes eye-to-eye with Monica.

"Are you okay? Too out of breath?" laughs Katherine.

"Yeah, I think so…"

"What are you doing tonight?"

Monica shakes herself, stretches her neck, yawns to unblock her ears.

"Nothing. Actually, I'm going to head home. I should really start to write my article. What about you?"

"Oh yeah! I'm supposed to help you, right? Hey, have you ever been to l'Escalier?"

"No, I don't think so. Or I'm not sure, maybe. What is it?"

"It's a bar not far from here, over there, across from

the Berri-UQAM metro station. If you're okay with it, if you drink, we could go have a beer or something. We could plan your article."

"Okay, yeah! Good idea, I'm in."

"It's this way!"

I don't know what's going on. Inside me something is rumbling, in the distance. There are rivers in my eyes. Where do they come from? I don't know how to go back upstream. For an instant, I'm breathing again. I don't know why I'm thinking of my mother.

For a long time, I resented my own existence. She'd already told me, several times, that she regretted having me. I always wonder if that was really possible, if she could really regret it.

Red dress.

Tearing.

If I keep going, if I keep going all alone, here, in Montreal, will I end up disappearing too, for good? Do I risk dying just by existing? Did my mother always run that risk too? Of disappearing?

Hammer.

There, in Sept-Îles, in the apartment where she lives today, maybe she remembers that being a mother is loving your child. Maybe she recalls her happy times with me. It was too long ago. Except that for her, the adult woman I have become is nothing, it doesn't matter. I'm not what she would have wanted me to be. The woman she imagined I would become. I don't even know what she thought. What justified her denying me, just because I exist.

A candle snuffed out.

The years she spent going out drinking, sometimes

staying out all night, leaving me alone at home. Was she running away from me? If not, from what, from whom? We were always at odds. I was always defying her. Always angry with her. And she was always upset because I was not a quiet child, as she told me. Always angry with me.

Her absences became my favourite moments. When I was alone at home. I could choose the breakfast I liked, cut my toast the way I wanted, sing the songs I wanted in the morning. Otherwise she controlled everything. Forbade everything. When I was alone, I watched what I wanted on TV. When she was there, I couldn't watch anything. I wasn't allowed to cook. I couldn't choose my clothes. Never, without her demeaning comments. As if she wanted to erase me.

Roses.

Was she made of something else, aside from that anger, that control? I don't know. With time, she became like a ghost. She was more and more afraid of the outside world, of other people looking at her; she isolated her-self...with me, at least. Yet when she had to go out, for groceries, for example, she was the one who demanded attention. She wanted the attention, she didn't want me to be the one who got noticed, complimented, cher-ished, loved.

Thorns.

Montreal. Montreal is my freedom. We are thousands, but we're alone, each in our own home. I have my apart-ment, where I do what I want. I'm far away from my past now. I came here without baggage, I left everything that tied me to her far behind, in Forestville.

I would like my throat to open up in a scream. I can't do it. I want to tear petals off roses too, to spit out thorns, tip over candles to put out the flames and spread the wax around, and finally throw pails and pails of water to flood the streets of my rage. I would shriek my own name. So that the past would change forever. I never wanted it anyway.

Fade to black.

The two women arrive at the bar after climbing the stairway that gave the bar its name, and Katherine looks around. Loud, pulsing music almost drowns out the buzz of conversations and laughter and the clinking of glasses on counters and tables. Everyone there seems to feel the excitement, as if they are in harmony with the ambient sound. Katherine walks over to the counter across from the entrance.

"Hiiiiii!" she says to the barman. "How are things going tonight?"

"Hey, hi there! Tonight? Same as always. I think it'll fill up soon. How are you doing?"

"Not bad. So, who's playing?"

"It's Native Night! Didn't you see that it's the first Thursday of the month?"

"Oh, yeah! Hey, Monica, good timing, there's going to be lots of people to introduce you to, you'll see."

Monica looks around. "Yeah, I didn't remember the name, but actually I do know the place, I've been here before… Last year, when I started classes, I came here to study a few times. But it's a little noisy for that! I think we're going to have trouble planning my article here, but it doesn't matter, I'll do it tomorrow during the day."

"What can I get you, ladies?"

"I'm gonna have an IPA. What about you, Monica?"

"Uh, the same."

"Okay, girls, coming right up!"

Katherine looks at Monica, who seems a little dazed. Monica scans the bar, like she's seeing it with new eyes. It's packed with people with all kinds of styles, who speak languages from everywhere in the world, excited, happy.

"Should we find a table?"

"Yeah, okay. Over there?" she says, pointing next to the stage.

After zigzagging through bags on the floor and the revellers already drinking, they sit down side by side at a tiny table with four chairs, each a different shape and colour. As they wait for their drinks, both automatically scroll through their phones. They add each other on Facebook and exchange phone numbers. A comfortable silence settles between them for a moment while they check out other tables, the people entering in waves. Then Katherine turns to Monica, to prepare her for what is coming.

"So, you know, tonight is the night when artists from all kinds of Nations usually come to perform and stuff. They do that every first Thursday of the month here. It's really nice, all kinds of people come out, but especially since it's Native Night, you know, it's our night! It's the place to be."

"Oh yeah? I'd never heard of it before."

"It seems like you don't know much, eh! I mean, it seems you don't know Innuat or other Indigenous people in the city."

"Yeah, well, true enough, I guess you're right."

"And at the university?"

"Not there either. And I don't think there're any in my program—"

"Christ! It's about time you got out!" Katherine laughs. "How long have you been in town anyway?"

"About, like, eight years."

"Eight years! Well then, it's not like you just got here! You're not wet behind the ears!"

"Zing! I was once, but no more than you, ha ha ha ha!"

"C'mon. I've been here for ten years, with just some short breaks in other cities. I'm even beginning to get stale!"

The waiter appears between them and, with a little smile, puts down a pint of IPA in front of each young woman. Pensively, Monica lifts her glass to take a first sip.

"I always feel like leaving, it's just that I don't know what to do. I don't know what I'd do if I went to Toronto or, like, Ottawa."

"Nah, Ottawa's really boring, I'm telling you. Toronto's cool, and if you ever think you'd be interested in Winnipeg or Vancouver, I can tell you that Vancouver is really, really nice! It's just…"

"What?"

"Well, there still aren't all that many Indigenous people here. Over there, you can run into all kinds of people like us in the street or at events, but it's just…I don't know, you run into more racism there. You just have to be ready for it."

"Is it that bad?"

"Yeah. That's what I'm saying, right? Sometimes it's tough, but you get used to it."

"You get used to it? What about here, do you see a lot of it? Racism against us, I mean?"

"Here? It's as if people don't know we exist, so…they kind of do nothing. But it depends. I'm talking about Montreal. Around Kahnawake, right, you can hear all kinds of vile stuff. It's still fallout from Oka, I think. In the Outaouais region too, in the Abitibi… On the North Shore too, I'm sure. Anyway, I've heard awful stories. You know, my mother has seen all kinds of stuff too, she's told me things. And the darker you are, the more you get nasty looks. Like it excludes people, and it's not acknowledged. In the other cities, it's really in your face, it's crude, it's almost earnest!" She laughs. "No, it's not funny. Anyway, it's different, I think. That's just me, that's what I think. That doesn't mean it's the same all the time. There's even a guy who told me he thinks it's the other way around! Anyway…" Katherine's smile fades, and she takes another sip of her beer.

Monica leans back in her chair, looking thoughtful.

"What're you thinking about?" Katherine asks.

"Nothing…I'm trying to remember what I've seen before."

"Well, but maybe you don't see it. My skin's so brown, you know…I feel it sometimes, people looking at me. In a city, I see it when they try to guess if I'm Latina or Indian from India! But here, people aren't used to seeing so many Indigenous people. For example, in Toronto, with my face and my skin, they know I'm Indigenous! In Winnipeg, I've been followed a couple times by security guards, in a drugstore, for example… It's as if they know too, right away. They know it, and they follow me because they're afraid I'll steal stuff. Ha ha ha… Aargh, you know! When I just want to buy my Kotex!"

"What! For real?"

"Sure! Monica, I think you're too pale. That's maybe partly why you haven't seen it so much. You even look white. So, like, you can go unnoticed."

Monica doesn't know how to name how Katherine's words make her feel. She takes another sip of her IPA, as if the cold beer can soothe the heat rising in her chest. At the same time, she tries to remember similar ideas or incidents from when she was younger, when she was with her mother. It's not really clear, as if there were nothing in that corner of her memory, or else just a vague presence. As if every thought she had then was shrouded in the shadow of her mother.

After a while, after checking the notifications on her phone, Katherine glances up at her. "Hey, Monica, you're quiet all of a sudden. Sorry, you know, I didn't want to hurt you, if that's what I just did. I'm real sorry if I rubbed you wrong way!"

"No, it's okay. It's just that…it seems like just by saying that to me, you made me understand something, you know."

"What's that?"

"I don't know… The fact that maybe I didn't experience things like that, and that means I don't see them? But now I hope I never walk past someone without seeing that, you know… I don't know… Aargh."

"It's okay, Monica, we can stop talking about it if you want. You really are a good person, I saw it right away. Soon you're gonna meet all kinds of new people. Think about that instead. I have friends coming, and people who are their friends. Usually, there are Innuat, Atikamekw, Anishinaabe like me, and Kanien'kehá:ka, Inuit…people from the south too. You'll see, I think it'll do you good. And you know, soon, I don't know who's going to sing, but you're gonna hear some music from our home, or your home! We'll see who it is!"

At the entrance, there are swinging doors, and the sound they make when they open is like something from a cowboy movie. At one point, the two young women automatically turn in that direction, and Katherine recognizes the two guys who just walked in.

"Hey! Justin!"

The young man reacts immediately to his name, turning his head from side to side, looking for where the voice is coming from.

"Over here, Justin!"

Katherine smiles so broadly that Monica can see her straight white teeth sparkle.

Justin finally sees her, motions to his companion to follow, and heads straight for Katherine. They kiss on both cheeks.

"How are you doing, Kath?"

"Okay, okay! This is Monica, she's from Pessamit. And, James, how are you?"

Justin kisses Monica in turn as he introduces himself. The two men wear black-and-blue windbreakers and black caps with the same brand name, Adidas, but not the same design. Justin has a small moustache, while James is clean-shaven.

"I'm okay, you? I heard you went back and frenched my best friend, hey!"

"Hey yourself! It's none of your business, James! Peter's my best friend too, and I'm allowed to kiss him if I want!"

They laugh, and the two others join in. It's been a long time since Monica has met people who laugh so much, so easily.

"Do you know who's playing tonight?" Katherine asks.

"I don't know," Justin replies, raising his eyebrows. "I heard it was a guy from Malio. It'll be cool. It'll do us good, a nice song from back home. Okay, I'll be right back, we're gonna go order some pints."

"Okay! See ya!"

Monica and Katherine watch them walk away.

"Did you catch that? Justin there is from Malio, and James, he's more from Mingan. They've been in Montreal for a couple of years, for school. They met here, and they've been together ever since."

The doors squeak again, and right away Katherine shouts and raises both arms. "Gaaaaab!"

The young man turns to look for whoever's calling, and his face lights up as he recognizes Katherine. Biting the inside of her cheek, Monica watches him come over. She's overwhelmed by meeting so many people in such a short time. Especially other Indigenous people. It's strange for her to feel both too familiar and too strange with her own people.

Gabriel is wearing bright colours, with complex, fascinating patterns.

"Gab! This is Monica, I just met her today!"

Monica and Gabriel are about to say hello when they suddenly recognize each other.

"Hey!" they say simultaneously.

"We were in the same art analysis course!" Monica laughs.

"Yeah! I always wondered if you were Indigenous, but I was too embarrassed to just come out and ask you. But then what happened? You stopped coming."

"Ha ha ha, you should have talked to me when you had the chance! Yeah, well…it's just, I'm trying something else these days. I'm going to take other courses."

"Okay, but you know, it's nice all the same!" Katherine interrupts.

"Yeah! It's really great to see you here anyway. Where

32

did you meet, you and Kath?" Gabriel pulls over a chair to sit down near them, almost between the two.

"At the contemporary art museum! We went to the Rebecca Belmore exhibition," Monica replies.

"Oh, yeah! I have to go see that, I haven't been yet."

"Don't you want to order something, so we can have a toast?" Katherine asks.

"Ah, totally! I should go to the counter," he answers, glancing at the lineup at the bar, which is getting longer and longer.

"Yeah, I don't think the waiter'll come by any time soon, with everyone who keeps coming in!" Monica says.

"All right, all right, I'm going!" Gabriel stands up, smiling.

"Gab's really great, I really like him," Katherine says to her friend with a laugh. "You won't get bored with him."

"I guess not! I did notice him too, in the class, but I didn't know how to talk to him."

Gabriel comes back to the table as soon as he has his pint of lager. Katherine, Monica, and he are soon roaring with glee again, cracking non-stop jokes that make them laugh so hard they can be heard on the other side of the bar, except that doesn't seem to bother anyone at all—quite the contrary. People are talking louder and louder, fuelled by the infectious joy of Indigenous laughter. In the background, the music from the loudspeakers often changes in style but is always upbeat and danceable: a succession of tunes—cumbia, electro, and pop—then the DJ puts on an acoustic album with various instrumental tracks. The sound atmosphere, Monica notes, is eclectic, inviting, and warm, in keeping with the bar's image, its walls painted with all kinds of designs, crazy colours next to wallpaper with a pattern she didn't even know existed. Everyone is welcome here, you can feel it. After about an hour, Justin and James join them at their table. Just in time, since among the people streaming through the swinging doors, they see the artist for the evening, making a grand entrance carrying his red guitar case, with a Warrior flag sticker—an emblem of Indigenous resistance during the 1990 Oka Crisis—clearly visible.

"Eric Vollant, nice! I really like his music," Katherine says excitedly. "I've seen him three or four times here already. He doesn't play often, which is a drag, but when he does, he can make us either want to dance the makusham all night long or else weep with him over his heartbreaks."

"Oh yeah? Eric Vollant, you said?" Monica asks, phone in her hand as she looks for info on him on the Internet.

"Yes, Eric Vollant!" Gabriel says. "I'm the one who booked him! He's really awesome."

"From Malio, huh?"

"Yeah, Maliotown! Cool, ha ha ha ha!"

"Have you ever been to Malio?" Gabriel asks Monica. "You must have been."

"Uh, no, when I was little maybe, but I don't really remember."

"Huh?" Gab says, surprised. "That's it?"

"Well, I grew up mostly in Forestville. We didn't go to Sept-Îles too often. I hardly ever went to Pessamit after I was eight, except in the summer when I went to visit my grandparents. And my mother, well…she was never into going there, that's all."

Gabriel notices Monica's discomfort and redirects the conversation tactfully. "I love Pessamit so much… Hey, the beach there, right? We used to make fires there, in the summer, with my friends!"

"Wow!" Katherine exclaims in turn. "You make me want to go there! It must be fantastic..."

"Well, it's almost summer, you know! Let's go then, all three of us."

A series of improvised guitar notes comes from the bar loudspeakers and the five young people immediately turn their attention to the stage. Eric sets up, and after a few seconds, he again tries a few guitar chords to test the sound. The music that was playing has been turned off. The tech guy then signals Eric and asks him to sing a bit into the mike. As Eric Vollant sings, Monica watches the stage intently. The singer is new to her, but at the same time the music feels familiar.

What is this in-between feeling? And yet she's already seen this kind of show. All the same, in a way she can't explain, she has a feeling of going through one initiation after another with Katherine. An initiation...or a return to something familiar but distant? Yes, in her early childhood, certainly, she spent time in this same world, that same atmosphere. She thinks she remembers her mother, who at the time was someone who loved being with people, who knew the artists from the communities, who loved being surrounded with friends and family... That was before she totally shut herself off. Before she moved with her daughter to Forestville, just before Monica started Grade 2. She took a job as a clerk in the convenience store farthest from the western entrance of the tiny town, in the direction of Pessamit.

Monica suffered a lot from that isolation, all the more because she was violently rejected, both in elementary and high school. She watched endless American teen movies, badly dubbed into French, but it was better than feeling lonely. She thought it was simply because she looked different, because she preferred to be alone, focusing on her drawing. She had deduced that hers was the fate of those who, for no particular reason, were born to be excluded. That she would never have the same chances as the others, she would simply have no chances at all. At the same time, she became convinced over the years that, as in the movies, since her journey was already strewn with pitfalls and solitude, she was destined for something exceptional.

I'd like to go back to the village and walk its streets again. Breathe in the fragrance of its trees when I get there, open the car windows and undo my seat belt. The effect of that scent courses through my body every time. It's like recognizing your mother's smell among thousands of women. My village is my mother. I have no other. Going home means going back to my peaceful childhood.

I want to throw myself into the arms of the past.

Ashini Street goes straight to the river, lined with places that are full of life. The presbytery and the church are still there, unmoving, loyal sentries on the shore, in the winds and tides. My grandparents' house and my uncle's house, side by side, bastions of my childhood summers. There, in the yard, my grandfather used to pluck partridges and hang them over a fire surrounded with big stones. He would stretch beaver pelts on frames made of branches, thread the sinews through the holes around the edges of the pelts to pull them tighter, and you could see the suppleness of the hide and the colours of the skin on the reverse, from pink to violet, like the hues of morning just before sunrise.

I'd like to be able to join him in the yard, cut through the little parking area to the left of the house, speak to him, see him turn toward me with his shining eyes, and I would walk softly toward him.

I'd like to tell him that I'm managing okay, that I'm looking for foundations, references, for a way in. I would like to be able to touch the beaver pelt again, feel the breeze rise as it welcomes the smell of fire and meat grilling. If I close my eyes, my dream will disappear.

If I go forward, I will fall into the night.

From time to time, the happy group bursts into laughter like a single chorus, enhancing the sound of the music. Vollant has just started the last song of his first set. The folk music, with a little country influence, makes the evening feel complete. The Innuat in the room in particular laugh so loudly that sometimes the singer smiles between two light notes. You can see he's not at all bothered by his rowdy audience.

Katherine and Gabriel start a conversation about common friends, and Monica looks away to listen more attentively to Eric's performance. The singer closes his eyes for a few measures, then opens them, and his pupils shine when he sees the room thrum in front of him. Monica gazes at him, twisting a strand of hair around her fingers. She sighs.

Justin, sitting very close to her, notices her discomfort and leans in close to her ear. "Do you understand?"

"What?"

"What he's singing?"

"Ah. I think I get bits of it… It's been a long time since I've heard Innu, you know."

Justin explains to her that the song is a humorous

retelling of the story of a painful breakup, mostly from the point of view of the singer. The second verse, more tender, is about how he'd like to take care of his little boy's mother, despite their separation, how generous she was to love him, how she supported him throughout his difficult adolescence. The song is an homage to a woman who had such a big impact on his life.

Monica is surprised to realize the extent to which she had understood the intent, even though she hadn't gotten all the words. No doubt because of the intonation, the melody…

"He's really good, that guy. He sings everywhere, in the communities. Sometime you'll have to go see him back home. It's definitely not the same as here, back there. Everyone loves his tunes. People really get off on it, they dance. You'd like that, I'm sure of it."

"Oh yeah? It's true that here we stay sitting at our tables, we listen…or don't listen! Ha ha!"

"Hah! Yeah, here, of course, it's not the same. Maybe because people don't know the makusham! Eh, ha ha ha!"

"Maybe that's all there is to it."

"Maybe, yeah, that must be it."

After a few words of greeting to the audience and a promise to come back in twenty minutes for the second set, Eric Vollant puts down his guitar and steps off the stage to join friends. Gabriel gets up to pass the hat to top up the artist's meagre fee. Monica, still laughing, turns toward the counter, wondering if she has time to get a pitcher for everyone during the break. People have been pouring in steadily since she and Katherine arrived, and those who were already there are also taking advantage of the break to order drinks. A throng of people chat, joking, almost shouting to understand one another, as music blares from the loudspeakers.

As she scrutinizes all those faces, trying to gauge who's trying to order and who's just hanging around, Monica starts. Something has just brushed against her ear, and she thinks she's heard a noise, a rustling, like the flight of a bird. She looks over at Justin, James, and the others, who are engrossed in their cheery conversations. Behind them, the window is wide open. Nothing. No one has been disturbed by anything. Monica again looks toward the entrance, and there she recognizes an unusual face among all those heads and bodies.

Sebastian.

It's been weeks since she's seen him. Weeks since she's been able to reach him. He hasn't answered her texts or her Facebook messages. Puzzled, a few weeks earlier she dared to ask a girl she knew was close to him, a singer who accompanied him sometimes on percussion, but she got only a vague answer. It was impossible to know where he was. He'd had a show in Toronto, then another in a bar in Montreal. He was back and forth between the two cities.

And now he's here. In the flesh.

She sees him greet his friends. Then he hugs two girls with long black hair, thick, perfect eyelashes, and high, glowing cheekbones, tight jeans. Sebastian, dressed in black, much taller than the other men around, appears even more majestic, undeniably beautiful, cloaked in mystery. Monica is struck by the same certainty as at their first encounter: he is magnetic. When he laughs it looks so natural, his head tilted back, his eyes disappearing behind two curved black lines. Everyone laughs with him. As soon as he moves, it's like people instinctively follow. All the energy in the room emanates from him, and converges on him, toward his body, toward his face in the crowd.

The floor seems to split in two to create a void under Monica's chair. Her legs stop tapping to the beat, and she goes cold, shivering. Her hands fidget on her knees.

She stands up. The free-flowing conversation at the table breaks off for a moment, and the others watch her walk toward the counter, before going back to drinking and exchanging barbs. There're so many people, too many people... She wants to go across the room, to the washroom. She'd like him to notice her. Monica doesn't feel like elbowing her way through to get close to Sebastian; she would look awkward, no. She chooses to go around through the different rooms of the bar before coming back to the entrance, under the pretext of going to the washroom, something, anything.

Walking slowly, dreading that meeting, that face-to-face, that exchange, she crosses one room after the other, blind to the crowd. With her whole being, she knows she shouldn't. But she's not equipped to neutralize the force that draws her in that direction, and she steps forward.

She counts the metres, her strides. She approaches the bottleneck, the narrow corridor at the end of which she knows she will find him. In a final instant of doubt, she freezes, but suddenly Sebastian is there, emerging from the pack. Sebastian, directly in front of her. She holds her breath. He looks her in the eyes for a moment. Monica's heart is pounding at the thought of all the possibilities. Without a word, Sebastian steps around her and walks off behind her.

After that, it's as if her spirit has left her. Nothing is

circulating in Monica's body. As if she's been flooded with cold. She turns slowly, wants to see him go, swallowed up by the crowd.

Four months earlier, in the depths of winter, she met him in a bar on Saint Denis Street. She'd gone in there by chance after seeing a film on architectures of the world with a girl from her class. She was supposed to take the bus farther on, at the corner of Sherbrooke Street, to go east, to go home. But she had decided to stop for a drink, just to avoid going home right away. And, in a way, to fill the emptiness she had been feeling.

She was quietly drinking her IPA at the counter. She liked to sit there, it was the perfect place to watch the world go by. To contemplate the people coming and going, partying or crying in their beer. To observe human beings and their dramas. To be still amidst their movement. Outside, it was a mild February night. It was getting to be about midnight when Monica, glancing out the window, noticed it was snowing, little flakes. The temperature must have fallen some. Monica was wearing ankle boots with thin soles, not great on slippery sidewalks. The plan was to finish her drink and leave.

She stood up from her stool just when he started singing a first, heart-rending melody. Etched in her memory.

He was standing onstage with his black guitar, his head bent forward, and his long, raven-black hair brushing against his shoulders, partly veiling his face. What she could see was a sad expression that powerfully echoed the loneliness Monica was feeling. Unsure of herself, she stayed motionless for an instant, simply admiring that image, a poet and his music. The lyrics of that first song, in English, felt like a poem to the young Innu woman;

41

they rang true, though she barely read any poetry. She knew that his words would follow her wherever she went.

> *I am here*
> *Looking for a nest*
> *To hold my skin*
> *And rest from my fears*

Yes, it was exactly that. As best she could, she was constructing a nest among the condos and the skyscrapers lined with fragments of her story. Decorated with pieces of driftwood, the only vestiges of the North Shore in her home. With leafy branches gathered on hidden paths, she had fashioned the walls of her inner house. Nothing more. Any wind could bring down a few timbers; her nest was like a house of cards. So she went back each time to the structure, tirelessly. Nothing solid, just what she needs to survive.

I am here...

Monica was still staring at the singer when he looked up for a moment and their eyes met. She instantly felt an electrical shock in her body, a warmth that rose in her chest and ran through her skull to the roots of her hair. She felt the tips of her fingers go cold. He closed his eyes, and a single chord ran through her body.

She almost lost her balance trying to get back on the stool she'd left a few seconds before. Embarrassed, she took a deep breath, leaned with her hands on the counter, and, when the barman walked by behind it, she took the opportunity to order another pint of bitter beer.

The very idea of leaving was gone from her mind, and she devoted the whole next hour to gazing at the singer, captivated by his understated performance, as he alternated interactions with the audience and songs interpreted with as much sweetness as melancholy. His voice husky, he shared his experiences of solitude or else poked fun at himself, engaging with the captivated, amused audience, his guitar emitting notes in warm colours that enraptured Monica. She felt so close to him, like they shared the same exile. From one song to the next, she wanted more and more to get close to him, to know him.

Looking for a nest...

He finished the last song, put down his guitar, and stepped off the stage to sustained applause. Several audience members were already walking over to him. Monica watched them. He had an enthralled audience here. Especially women, of all ages. He drew them into his orbit as surely as the sun, she thought, seeing all those ladies beg for a smile, for an instant of his attention, hoping for a conversation. He seemed so shy and so pleasant at the same time. He answered them all with heartfelt empathy. After a while, he managed to extricate himself from the little crowd and went over to the counter. Monica's heart started beating a little faster and, once again, a wave of warmth ran through her body. He came to order something, very close to her. She kept her head straight, looking toward the windows, through which the snow greeted her shining eyes. She heard the barman ask what his headliner wanted to drink, then enthusiastically pour the pint of IPA. Monica, transfixed, didn't know what to do. A growl was shaking up all her senses, and in her head she tried to come out with a first phrase, a comment, any strategy to approach him. Maybe she should make a remark to him about their shared love for bitter beer? No.

To hold my skin…

"Hey…"

His voice filled Monica's ears with tenderness. She turned her eyes toward him, unsure of what was happening. Yes, he was talking to her. Her blood started running through her whole body like lightning slicing through a cloud. Her hands were clammy.

"Are you enjoying your evening?" he asked in English.

Taken aback, Monica searched the room around her before answering. "Oh shit, me? Sorry…I…I don't really speak English…"

He smiled even more broadly. He gazed deep into her eyes and took a sip of beer without looking away. "It's okay… Je…parle un peu le français…"

"Ah! Yes, we can try speaking in both languages… I just… I have to speak more…"

"I guess we'll figure it out," he laughed. "Je vais pratiquer…aussi."

By way of an answer, Monica returned his smile. She was thunderstruck and didn't know what to add. His entire performance had been in English, but somehow the language barrier was as unexpected as it was predictable. She wouldn't have imagined hearing him speak to her in French, and with that accent that melted her heart… She was suddenly faced with questions: *What should I do? Communicating will be quite a challenge! If we were to have children, what language would they speak first? What school would they go to?*

Monica! she scolded herself, amused to find herself already imagining an entire life with him.

Keep it simple! One thing at a time.

And rest from my fears…

Yes, one thing at a time.

Leaning against the l'Escalier bar, Monica is suddenly thirsty. She regains her composure and observes her new friends, at a distance, while she slowly comes back into her body, her mind emerging from the past. Katherine is looking back at her, her expression full of questions. *What's going on? What are you doing?*

Monica puts off her plan to order a pitcher and heads back to the table, avoiding the entrance and the group Sebastian seems to be with. She wonders if someone who's already seen them together would recognize her, but no, no one notices, no one speaks to her.

Back at the table, she turns her attention—what's left of it—to Gabriel, while he tells joke after joke to Justin and James. They provide an ideal audience for his extravagant humour.

Katherine, for her part, tries to maintain visual contact with Monica, guessing the weight of shame behind her lowered eyes. She recognizes that reaction all too well. She only needs to know what, or who, is the cause. Monica had said she didn't come here often, she didn't know the crowd… Katherine, apparently not one for guessing games, blurts out her questions.

"Monica, what's the matter? Did the barman say something stupid to you?"

Monica looks up, taken aback. "Not at all. Why?"

Lowering her voice to avoid attracting the attention of the others, Katherine probes further. "Don't put on your little Pessamit seashell act, I can see there's something. What just happened?"

"Nothing, I'm telling you."

Monica thinks for a moment, chewing on her cuticles nervously, while Katherine shakes her head in protest.

"Monica! I want to be your friend, and if you trust me,

you can tell me everything. It's no big deal, I've already heard everything... I've gone through all kinds of things! You know, there's nothing you can say that you should be embarrassed to tell me, if that's what's stopping you. Did you puke on the bathroom floor?"

"Look, you know, it's nice of you, but I have nothing to say, there's nothing to tell. I...I...I'm a bit tired, I talked with like a hundred and fifty people I don't know tonight, plus I just remembered I haven't written my article yet, so that's stressing me out, that's all. I'm going to go soon, I think."

At the counter, a little group starts talking loudly and doing shooters off a tray. Laughter erupts each time someone knocks back a drink to shouts of encouragement. The racket attracts Katherine's attention, and she recognizes a face, a singer who is widely known in the urban Indigenous community, and especially among anglophones. They say no one can resist him, that he is an exceptional artist, a creator whose melodies are full of shadows and light that no one can imitate and everyone admires. When he sings, he breaks hearts. He even overshadows Eric Vollant when they share the stage. But Katherine has a different take.

Over the years, several of her closest friends have been mistreated by the notorious Sebastian. Katherine finally saw through his game, endlessly repeated... Each time he joins a new circle of friends, he charms all the girls. He makes those who fall for him believe he's crazy about them. He goes out with them for months, two or three at a time, each one bragging: *I'm the one who's dating him, I'm in love with him, he told me he loves me. We love each other!*

Except that the Indigenous world is small, very small.

It's sometimes led to fights between women in the bars where he goes and from which he always runs away at the right time. Some of his conquests have been destroyed by this, too hurt, unable to put things in perspective.

Katherine herself had to put a stop to the rumour that she too had a relationship with him, when, in fact, she's kept her distance since the first evening she saw him circling his prey. She finally found out that the gossip was the work of a former friend who didn't understand why Katherine had come between her and Sebastian, and concluded that it was because Katherine was keeping him for herself.

Disgusted by his duplicity, by the pain he leaves in his wake, she feels only one thing for him now: she wishes that he would fall from his pedestal, that he would regret his actions one day, one way or another. She hasn't forgotten to what extent, before knowing what kind of man he was, she loved that artist. She could have fallen at his feet too. His charm is dangerous. God knows what he's done to others. No one has denounced him so far. No one speaks out. And that enrages Katherine every time she thinks about him.

She glances again at Monica, who now seems lost in the bottom of her glass, cut off from the world, inaccessible. Katherine doesn't know for sure what's happening to her or what's on her mind, but she worries as she studies her new friend's face. Her lustrous black hair, so shiny that it sparkles red under the lights, her eyebrows extending like wings above her expressive eyes, her cheekbones round and high… She's feeling something that scares her.

If Monica ran into Sebastian, he'd try to seduce her. And Monica, who seems a bit lost and innocent, wouldn't be able to avoid getting caught in the grip of that snake.

The group gravitating around Sebastian fortunately heads to another room in the bar, finally clearing the way and allowing others to line up to order. Monica looks up and heads to the counter, Katherine on her heels.

"What do you want?" Monica asks her.

"Well, the same thing. But didn't you want to go home?"

"Soon, not right away. I'm gonna get a pitcher. You want a shooter too?"

Katherine stares at Monica for an instant, perplexed, while her friend scans the menus on the blackboards above them. "Jameson."

"Perfect."

"Yeah, I'm sorry I didn't help you more after all! But anyway, I hope you're not sorry we came. How are you finding it?"

"Yeah, no, it doesn't matter. For the article, I'll just have to say that I came to see the Indigenous cultural evening after the exhibition, to make a connection between the two events, and then I'll send it tomorrow night. It's really nice, Eric has some great tunes. I found his site just now. I'm going to listen to his stuff online, of course."

"Yeah, for sure, I listen to his albums all the time at home... Everywhere I go, in fact! Hey, we could come up with a routine to one of his songs and start a TikTok challenge with that! Ha ha ha!"

Without answering, without even smiling, Monica leans on the counter and orders. With a protective reflex, Katherine checks whether there are any shadows lurking. For the time being, she doesn't notice anything. She doesn't know, cannot know, that Monica, at the same time, moves a bit to the side, deliberately trying to get within range of Sebastian.

Except that he and his group of friends have found a table behind a low wall, farther away in the backroom. Monica can see him, but he can't see her. His whole group appears to be having a great time. Some are singing songs, which leads to bursts of laughter, others stand up to tell jokes, their expansive movements intensifying the euphoria. She realizes he's hiding, but she can't believe it's because of her. Maybe he drank too much and didn't recognize her... Or else, as she has already witnessed, he's hostage to those who consider themselves his friends but who are there only for his name, his aura. Maybe even, as often happens, a few fans wanted to join them after a show he performed somewhere else, and they keep following the group, and that's why Sebastian is so evasive... She comes up with reasons. Skirts the truth. Her heart is at loggerheads with her head.

Don't do anything, don't move!

But I want to see him, to get him to see me. To get him to come to me, like the very first time, to join me, me, me alone, at the back of the bar and, yes, if it ever seems possible, we'll have a drink together again. To get him to do that again, to put his arm around me and pull me to him, while our pints and our shooters pile up like bodies on the table in front of us. And—

Monica, no!

Katherine, seeing Monica preoccupied, grabs the drinks, then hands her the whisky before leading her to their table, pitcher in her hand. Once the two women have returned to their companions, the evening continues, one glass after another. Monica is enjoying the diversions provided by Justin, James, Gabriel, and Katherine. It's been too long since she's laughed like this. These last weeks, all she could do was try to survive the pain that gripped her as soon as she thought about Sebastian's absence, his silence. She's never been abandoned, ignored that way, by anyone. Other than her mother.

Deep inside, twigs from her nest tumble to the ground, but on the outside she's smiling broadly, laughing with her new friends. With all her strength, she clings to the idea that perhaps they will become close, and she'll be able to see them from time to time, become a friend, an important friend, a friend who is loved, who is not abandoned.

Monica, drunk now, looks at Katherine, who is weeping with laughter. Justin and James are born comedians.

Katherine is remarkable. She might have strong opinions, but they seem enlightened and relevant. When Katherine expresses herself on issues that affect the communities specifically, Monica wishes she herself had a little more knowledge about the First Peoples—the term Katherine asks people to use. *It's decolonial, we will not be defined according to the terms of the descendants of settlers, and because we were the first ones here!* She would definitely agree with her new friend. It bothers her to have so much trouble taking part in these conversations, to realize she really doesn't know much about her own Nation, and even less about others.

She blames her mother for that. She built walls around the two of them that cut Monica off from the possibility of having more playmates—and ensured she had even fewer Innu friends. For Monica, it seemed incomprehensible, violent. She felt so isolated, surrounded by nothing and no one, having to make do with the sole presence of her mother, who seemed too caught up in the web of her own thoughts and inner struggles to do anything other than leave her daughter alone, with her toys, the board games she could not play by herself, and later her sketchbooks, or dancing to songs she heard on the radio. Her solitude.

After each sip and each new glass, the alcohol seems to instantly ease the pain that keeps surfacing. The second set has been over for a while, and Monica realizes it's almost three in the morning. Everything is easy, everything is light.

She once again feels bird wings beating close to her, so hard this time that she jumps in her chair.

Katherine, tipsy, starts laughing. "What's wrong now, Monica? Ha ha ha! You're bouncing around like crazy!"

"I was startled, I thought there was someone behind me."

More laughter. That reminds Justin of another anecdote, which he starts to recount with great enthusiasm and a string of comical imitations to colour the characters of his story.

Monica turns around. She has the impression she recognizes that feeling, that shiver running down her neck.

She looks for him, and he appears at the corner of the hallway.

She stands up. Determined, she walks over to him, accompanied only by her pain, which throbs and pulses. He's put on his leather coat and slung his backpack over his right shoulder. He ends his conversation with a person Monica does not see, turns around, and notices her heading straight toward him. With long strides, without hesitating more than a second, he heads quickly to the stairway leading outside. The animal has been roused and too swiftly takes flight.

But Monica refuses to let the opportunity to understand go by and follows him down the stairs. "Sebastian!"

At the foot of the staircase, she pushes open the glass door and steps outside. No one. Black feathers are scattered across the asphalt. A car drives by. There is only the noise from the open doors of the metro station across the street, like the song of a humming generator that fills the moment with its indomitable presence, but Monica perceives nothing other than the absence of the Raven.

How is that possible? Has he been staying away on purpose all along? What happened? What did I do?

Brushing aside the dizzying thoughts, she turns her attention to what she has so much trouble believing, though it's plain as day: he just ran away from her! He saw her, she's sure of it because she was able to look deep into his eyes, their dark void. Just long enough to feel the intensity of the bond between them, which she can't live without.

Tears are streaming down her cheeks. She imagines Sebastian's touch on her hand. She had locked away every detail of a night when they went walking on a little bridge over the Lachine Canal, in the southwest of the city. One of their first moments together. She had met up with him in a bar near there. A little before dawn, they finally ended up at her place, in the east end. She sat in his lap and they shared a can of beer while he squeezed her tight. Then, without getting up, they touched each other for a long time in silence, until he picked her up in his arms to take her to her bed, and there they melted into each other's arms. Around seven o'clock, he got up to leave. She couldn't get back to sleep and stayed there alone, without knowing who she could call to share the joy and the turmoil she was feeling. To talk about that love that was being born, taking root within her.

She had never really been able to make real friends.

Since she'd lived in the city, she'd barely been able to make minimal connections with other members of her department at the university. The presence of Sebastian in her life was all she had that was concrete, genuine, the only thing of value. She just had to be patient until the day their relationship could become more stable, since he was travelling a lot for his music. That's what she told herself as she started the coffee maker on mornings when she felt lonely.

As Monica broods over her memories, the street seems to have slowed down, the sounds muted. She's been outside for five minutes, waiting, in case he reappears. Suddenly, with an infernal racket, Katherine comes crashing downstairs, almost running into Monica, who is still standing right in front of the door, bathed in the glow of the street light.

"Hey! This is where you were! What the hell..."

Monica closes her eyes, tries to hold back her tears before opening them again.

"Monica, okay, there's something for sure, tell me what's going on! I can tell you're not all right." As she speaks, Katherine puts her hands on her friend's shoulders, tries to revive their budding connection by shaking her.

"No, it's nothing, I told you! Let go of me!" Monica says, shaking herself free.

"Monica, please!"

With angry energy, Monica opens the door and goes back up the stairs, wiping her eyes and her cheeks. She doesn't want Gabriel, Justin, and James to see what she's just gone through.

"Hey, Monica! You're back! You looked lost when you left! Katherine even went to see where you went off to like that, without your phone!"

"Yeah, I wasn't feeling right for two seconds," she laughs. "I went to get some air."

Katherine takes her time coming back upstairs. That gives her a few moments to cool down a little. She's been trying her best to support her new friend, but Monica doesn't seem to want her help. At the top of the stairs, she glances around the bar. No trace of Sebastian.

Back at their table, Katherine is pensive. She grabs her glass but stays standing, one hand on her hip. She knows she has a reputation as the kind of friend who protects those she loves, whether they want it or not. More than anything, she would like to prevent broken hearts, illusions, lies, but most often she resigns herself to playing the counsellor after the worst has happened, and she always applies herself to the task willingly, even though she knows her suggestions won't necessarily be accepted. But what if the handsome, predatory singer is mixed up in this story?

Monica, who's far gone enough that she's already forgotten their argument down on the street, draws Katherine out of her thoughts by handing her another full glass, stumbling. "To this day, my friend!"

Two glowing red lines go past me, very close, and across the huge field in which I stand. It's nighttime. There are no stars. The only light in the cloudless sky are these red beams. The field is the one behind my house, the vacant lot of my childhood. Where, each year, spring scatters its dandelions, and swarms of bees continue the cycle of whispers, the whispers of the wings shining subtly on their backs, in secret dialogue with the sun, the flowers, the rodents.

That's where I walk to go to school. Where winter came and piled icy mountains twenty times the height of the neighbourhood children, where the storms were blizzards from the north and we felt like we had already reached the sky for the first time, everything was so immaculate all around. When I was little, at night, I dreamed the dark was so deep that I never managed to get home after school, I couldn't find the path through the high grass. Now I'm in that same dream. I'm an adult. I'm lucid too. But something else is different… New red lines appear and cross the whole field. As they pass, a dull noise. Again. As if those lines, those streaks of light, were giving off something like the sound of the electrical cables strung from the hydro towers.

The red lines increase in number, flat as the ground and the sky, and I stand still. I don't know if I should keep moving forward, at the risk of coming into contact with burning beams of light. I think I should, and I start to walk again, though I avoid touching them. I take a step forward. I can still walk between the two beams stretching out on either side of me. Everything is sinister, frightening. Except the air is cool and fresh. I breathe. I hear a voice. A woman shouts my name. It sounds like my mother, twenty years ago, when she was looking for me from high up on the balcony, when she expanded her lungs to call me.

"Monica!"

I don't know if she knows I'm an adult now. I didn't know she had returned to live in that apartment, with all those weighty memories. Those lungs seem to have been hand-drawn to take flight in the black sky, from the place where my childhood apartment building stands, to my right. Her lungs float quietly in the air, pushed by a breeze. There's no rush, no one is panicking. What should I do? My mother's lungs fly into the air. Should I jump? Blue and red veins wave around bronchial tubes.

I pick up speed between the fluorescent lines and feel a power within myself that I know will allow me to reach the sky, and then I start floating too. I try to reach them. Not yet. I rise and I rise, I move like I'm running, but in the air, and I sense, yes, gravity, though at the same time it seems non-existent... I take my eyes off the flying lungs for an instant to look down, and the red lines, their strong glow, span the whole field from one end to the other. They form strange patterns. Double curves. The view is mesmerizing, and I lose myself contemplating it.

Then it comes back to me. The lungs. I have to catch them. I look around and realize I've gone too high. The night surrounds me, I feel its warmth gently envelop me. In the distance, I see that the lungs are still floating, but they're heading toward the luminous rays in the field, losing altitude. I'm over here. Far away. I look up, search for stars: there are none. It's like a ceiling, so close to my head and so dense that it seems there is only dark infinity before me. That's what's touching me, like a blanket that someone has gently draped over my shoulders. From up here, as I feel sleep come over me, I contemplate the lines on the ground. Their red light is soothing, reassures me, and I close my eyes. I hear a flapping of wings, thundering, and everything goes black.

The alarm buzzes. Monica can barely open her eyes. She can't see anything. She feels around her bed for her phone. Takes a few seconds to find it among her sheets.

Seven oh one. Too early. Too early, but time seems so slow. Almost solid. Too heavy to move forward. Monica turns over in bed. Her head is throbbing, as if it contains her swollen heart. In her deserted chest, everything is black. She opens her mouth to breathe better. Breathes in for a long time. Breathes out, strong. Tries to free herself from the pressure in her muscles.

In her mind, Sebastian's lustrous hair, his arms, his shoulders, his face. The laugh that gave her shivers, how it resonated in her. His dark eyes, gemstones cut in the night. She had lacked the words to describe him. The scientific reasons to explain the sensations that swept over her each time his body moved, when he laughed or was even simply talking with people. Especially when he sang.

She remembers a time she went to meet up with him right after a class, when he was playing in a bar downtown. It was at the very beginning of their relationship. Monica's stomach was full of butterflies. When she walked into the pub, the set had just begun, Sebastian was warming up with his first measures, and when he spotted her under the stage lights, his eyes suddenly seemed to shine stronger.

I'll always remember that instant, she had whispered to him in her mind. *Don't let me ever forget every second of joy that you gave me,* she asked him again. That moment when in his eyes she could live, exist, breathe—she never wanted to forget it. She wanted him to always look at her that way. She had never been desperately in love, not like in the movies, so she couldn't have sworn that's what it was. But what she felt for him, from the very first day, was so intense that she sometimes felt that she couldn't go on, that that fever would burn her up completely. She told herself that must be it, true love.

She dozes. Falls back asleep, then wakes up again.

The day crawls along. Monica has no plans to get out of bed. Behind her curtains, the sun has come out and shines brightly. Monica's body feels heavy. She hurts everywhere. Her chest is so tight that her lungs have a hard time inflating when she wants to take a deep breath. She sighs, emptying her lungs to fill them again. She clings to the best memories of the day before. Katherine. Gabriel, Justin, and James. Their companions from all those nations who came by their table during the evening. A new universe. Another rotation of the world.

Except she knows very well that Sebastian's last act, scorning her as if she were a piece of roadkill, is draining her so completely that she has no desire to get up, to go out today. She wants to stay right there, without moving, nowhere.

Her phone rings. Monica rolls over. The ringing persists. Monica turns over again in her sheets and hides her head under her pillows. She resigns herself to opening her eyes to find her phone. She feels around with one hand but can't see anything since her thick locks are covering her eyes. The chaos is even in her hair. She brushes it off her face, her hand still unsteady.

It's a quarter past noon. It's Friday. Who could be calling?

Monica answers with a woolly *Hello?* It's Katherine, her voice cheerful but with a trace of the excesses of the night before.

"Kuei miam a? Ha ha. That's what you say in your community, right?"

"Yes, that's right," Monica answers hoarsely.

"Sorry, we said I'd sleep at your place, but I went

home in the end. I brought you home, and I kept the cab to go to my place. I really wanted to change my clothes to go to bed."

"Why's that? A little accident?" Monica laughs.

"Yeah! Ha ha! Yeah, in the taxi, it happens to me sometimes! No, I was just too hot yesterday, walking all over the city before going to the museum. And after, you know, we partied too hard, so I felt pretty rotten."

"Right, I get it. You make me laugh!"

"And you? How are you feeling this morning? Do you want to go for breakfast?"

"Oh, Katherine, I don't know…"

"It's true, you sound like a zombie! I'll come over to your place then. I'm in fine form myself. And I'm hungry. Do you have anything to eat?"

"Yes, all kinds of stuff… You can make me something to eat."

"Deal! Okay, I'll grab a cab, and I'll be right there. Okay? You can stay in bed if you like, I'll take care of everything. Just unlock the door! See ya!"

At home, Katherine hangs up and grabs her huge handbag. She throws in her phone, her keys, and a few other essentials for a day after a night out, such as sunglasses and painkillers. She had really wanted, earlier that morning, to stay with Monica, wake up with her, not leave her alone. She really looked like she was in bad shape. After her strange disappearing act outside, Monica had drowned herself in alcohol until closing time. She had started partying with a different energy, insatiable.

Katherine can't say for sure, but embers of doubt are smouldering in her gut, waiting only for some confirmation to set her anger on fire. Maybe this won't be easy.

Maybe it'll take a long time. Monica seems to want to keep it a strict secret.

There's still a chance that she's wrong. Hopefully she's wrong. He has already broken so many. Strong women. Women of the future. Women for rebuilding the Nations.

What she knows is that she loves her new friend. She's really funny, and she carries something inside her that Katherine cannot describe. But Katherine recognizes the baggage. A vital force. A will to discover, to live. To know. To be.

Yes, a strong woman of the future. And for that, you mustn't let ravens come and take your heart.

I didn't come seeking knowledge.
Neither to seek nor reflect.
I came here because I needed a place that could contain
my emptiness.
Again this morning—and yesterday, and tomorrow
—the cars go by, I hear their song. The trucks blur the
sound waves with their strident cries. The firefighters
can't put out the absence. The police can't muzzle
the blood beating in my temples.
My heart on strike.
I've lost track of the days.
Nights pass, and the stars fall from my hands.
What am I doing?

Monica in the middle of the party. Another one. With Katherine, you never get bored. It's time to live it up. To breathe. To breathe in the smoke of joints and cigarettes. To get drunk on the beautiful, heady aroma of strong alcohol. There's still time to finish the cases of beer. There's still time to run and kiss someone. The loveliest of the lovely on this new, seemingly endless night.

Monica turns around. Through the haze of the party, she spots Katherine languidly kissing a non-Indigenous woman. Monica's eyes seem to blur for a moment. The last shooter is having its effect, a buildup of warmth in her body. She closes her eyes.

Before the party ends, in the crowd gathered around Katherine, the animal with big black wings and red eyes appears among the boys and girls wrapped in smoke and music. He shouldn't have come. He wasn't invited. But through word of mouth, everyone ends up at the party. And Monica was expecting him anyway, as she always does, wherever she is, even when it's impossible for him to be there. When he suddenly appeared in the hallway just as Monica was taking a deep drag from a cigarette, his silhouette took her breath away. A shock wave ran through the group who were dancing. Wide, mischievous smiles appeared on all lips. Eyes went dreamy. The room suddenly became hot. *Yes, it's him, you've really seen him, it's that singer, his soul is so dark, the one who sings sad ballads that make everyone cry. As for me, I want more.*

Monica could no longer hear the music, the melancholy lyrics of Chris Isaak's "Wicked Game." Sebastian scanned the room, his eyes searching. He spotted Monica slipping closer, a furtive shadow coming closer to meet him, his lips.

The Black Bird responded by sticking his tongue between her teeth. She was his. At any rate, for one more night.

Tu m'aimes-tu?

Noon again. Do you love me? The question rings out on Monica's clock radio, which she hadn't heard when it came on earlier.

Richard Desjardins is singing, *t'es tellement, tellement, tellement belle*—you're so, so, so beautiful—and she wants so much for someone to say it to her too, she wants him, the Raven, to say it to her, yes.

Sebastian opened the door to the balcony off Monica's bedroom and lit a cigarette, leaning on the railing, watching people go by on the sidewalk below. Monica's cat went out to join his meditation.

Back inside the apartment, Monica, still lying on her bed, thought her lover looked more than ever like a bird, bent over the world, his back curved and black. Like the ravens that follow the comings and goings of humans on the sidewalks with curious eyes. Especially the women. Monica's mother was in the habit of jeering at them, chasing them away, reminding her daughter that corvids are scavengers that lie in wait for the sick and the weak. An idea drawn from all the Catholic stuff that they got her to swallow without question, and that she was still trying, back then, to instill in her daughter. But Monica found the ravens so beautiful, and nothing could convince her to find them nasty or threatening.

The sun made its appearance in the east, and she watched her Raven in the pale light, his hypnotic movements.

The sweetness of a June morning. Clear sky. Sebastian studied the street, puffing on his cigarette, while Monica kept her eyes on him, on his outline blurred by condensation on the window. She felt a touch of acidity in her stomach. Anxiety at the idea of letting him leave again. She didn't know what to do. Again. Always letting him go. Not holding him back. Not even getting an answer to why he had avoided her the other evening in the bar. The question didn't even pass her lips. But yesterday, he had chosen her again, that was the most important thing.

Watching the stooped shoulders of the man leaning on the balcony railing, Monica superimposed giant wings grafted onto his shoulder blades, black and majestic.

She's seen that silhouette many, many times in dreams over the last two years. She never saw the face in her dreams, couldn't even make out the precise shape—a human, some giant creature?—but what she knows is that when she saw Sebastian for the first time, she suddenly felt she recognized him. It was him.

Monica keeps her eyes closed to see better.

There's a persistent pounding on the door that locked automatically behind Sebastian when he left, with a promise, *keep in touch*. On the other side of the door is Katherine, completely hungover, in a panic.

Desjardins's song is playing in a loop in Monica's head. She clings to it as she does to the Raven. What she is feeling is huge. She sees herself in him, a soulmate.

"Monica! Open up!"

Katherine is knocking louder and louder, as if her fist were beating on the fear growing in Monica's belly.

Monica has not yet shared that feeling with him. That they are alike. She doesn't know how he would react. For the time being, it's enough for her to hold the belief deep inside and to suppress the miserable feeling that's trying to invade her heart, her throat, her head, each time he runs off in the morning.

The door is shaking under the repeated blows, curious neighbours are starting to poke their heads out on the landing, when finally Monica decides to get out of bed.

In her dark dressing gown, she walks painfully to the door, unlocking it with one hand.

Katherine bursts in. "Monica! Who did you go home with, huh?"

"What? What's your problem?"

"Monica, just tell me who you went home with!"

"Why are you asking me that? You show up here and you don't even say hello."

"No, Monica, you don't understand. There're guys you shouldn't bring home with you. And I feel responsible because you were at my place, at my party, and…"

Monica feels her stomach tighten. "Oh, come on, why are you saying that, Katherine?"

"Monica, I know I was drunk as hell, but I swear I saw him come into our place when he isn't fucking welcome, that bastard! I saw you kissing him! But someone came to get me because the damn toilet wouldn't stop running… and when I came back, you were gone!"

"Kath! Calm down! Nothing serious happened… I just needed—"

Katherine punches the wall next to her.

Monica shuts up. Katherine's reaction is excessive, scary. She doesn't dare say the name of the Raven.

"Look, it's really none of your business. Anyway, it wasn't at your place that we met, it's just that it had been a while… But, you know, that's the way it is, with Sebastian—"

"Shit, I knew it!"

"What do you mean? You know him? Have you seen him play?"

"Ah, Monica, goddammit… Will you believe me if I swear to you on my mother's head that Sebastian isn't a guy you want to be with?"

Her words make Monica's blood boil, and she spins on her heel and goes to the kitchen sink, pours herself a glass of water, her back to Katherine. "What do you know about it? What is it, have you slept with him?"

"No! It's not that, dammit! It's just that… Listen, Sebastian, he has hurt friends of mine a lot. Like, they were never right after."

"Come on, don't exaggerate. And besides, I don't really feel like listening to your ancient history. We're together, and I'd like you to respect that."

Katherine is stunned, falls silent for a moment. "Shit, Monica…"

"What?"

"How long have you been seeing him?"

"Stop it! I for one want a coffee, I'd like you to give me time to make it. And I'd like to take an Advil too, I have one hell of a headache."

"Okay, first things first, stop the pain. You're right,"

Katherine answers, digging in her purse, which she still hasn't put down, and taking out the vial containing her favourite medication.

"And you, come to think of it...I saw you kissing somebody all evening! Who was that woman? You didn't tell me you were seeing someone. You sneaky bitch!" Monica goes over to the counter and opens a cupboard to take out a jar of ground coffee. She puts a filter in the machine, while Katherine watches absent-mindedly.

"Ah, LOL. That was Laurence."

"Oh, Laurence, huh? Did you know her before?"

"Well, no!" Katherine laughs. "I met her yesterday, at the party, I don't know who invited her. It was really nice, we ran into each other by the sound system, and we started chatting about music. It turned out we had a lot of things in common, so we just spent the evening together, drinking, smoking. Then we went to do shooters in the kitchen. And anyway, well, that's that."

"Nice! Are you going to see her again?" Monica asks as she pushes the button to start the coffee maker. The question is intended to be nonchalant, but there is tension in her voice, a reaction to Kath's whirlwind arrival.

"Well, we friended each other on Facebook, and we texted each other our phone numbers. So...I guess we will."

"That's cool, I'm happy for you. It happens all the time that you meet someone like that at a party, and you realize you have all kinds of things in common."

Since Monica still has her back to her, Katherine doesn't know if her friend is just saying that or if she's making conversation to avoid revisiting her warning about Sebastian. Maybe she did come on a little too strong, she thinks, and plays along. "Yeah, that really feels good, it really does. Plus, while she's not Indigenous, she knows all kinds of things about what's going on out west, and she talked to me about them without necessarily whitesplaining to me. That's sexy, I think, someone who doesn't talk to you like they know more about you than you do yourself… Anyway, I like it a lot more when someone is respectful for real and isn't patting themself on the back with everything they know about us."

"Man, she really had an effect on you!"

When Monica finally turns around, Katherine looks her straight in the eye. "But you, Monica Hervieux… How long have you been seeing he who shall not be named?"

Monica says nothing. Katherine is so determined, so passionate when she talks about Sebastian, even when she's trying to be funny, to take the edge off. Her own face is expressive, quite clearly reflecting her discomfort, so Katherine can hardly ignore that she is hurting.

"Not so long…"

"Be honest with me, please! Fuck, I'm not here to judge you, you know!"

"Well, you came in here asking who I'm sleeping with!"

"Yeah, but, Christ, I saw him, that evening in l'Escalier, when you were being completely weird, and then I saw you leave with a guy who looked a hell of a lot like him! I was sure it was him, I wasn't that wasted, though maybe you were. So I'm entitled to want to know if my friend left with a nasty guy!"

"Okay, we've been seeing each other for four months. You're pissing me off!"

"What the fuck." Katherine's jaw drops.

"So what?"

"Four months, like since February?"

"Yeah."

"Shit."

"Whaaaat!"

A long beep indicates that the coffee is ready. Monica takes the opportunity to turn her back on Katherine again and busies herself preparing two cups of coffee.

Katherine's tone softens. "Monica, that guy, he's destroyed so many of my friends, I swear to you. He's a dangerous man. A manipulator. How many times have you seen him in four months, really?"

Monica, who is pouring the coffee into the second cup, stops abruptly.

"Monica?"

Silence.

"Hello!"

"Okay, I don't know, like four or five times..." Katherine's friend answers shamefully. She doesn't feel like going into details. Nor does she want Katherine to realize that Sebastian has just left, that if you look closely, you can still see fine black feathers in the corners of the apartment.

"Four or five times!"

Monica, retreating into silence, adds almond milk and a spoonful of cane sugar to each of the cups.

"Monica...just four or five times in four months?"

"I know, okay!"

Katherine looks sadly at Monica. She feels powerless, with everything she knows about that man... She finds it overwhelming. If only she and Monica had met sooner. She felt it, in the bar that time, the change in her friend's behaviour as soon as he appeared, but she didn't want to believe it, especially since he didn't seem to know her.

She saw him walk right past her, completely ignoring her. But she obviously misinterpreted his action. Typical of him, of a man who uses others. Typical of a manipulator. Cowardly and stupid.

"I swear to you, he does that to everyone. A man like that can destroy a woman. He can make you believe that you're a couple if you've slept with his shadow three times in a year."

"Okay, Katherine, I get it!"

"I just want to tell you the truth! I find it so, so… frustrating to know that he got to you. That's it. It happened, I can't do anything about it. All I can do is freak out and tell you the truth."

On top of her pounding headache, Monica is feeling worse and worse. Each additional word Katherine says about Sebastian makes her shudder. As if something were yielding in her body. Except she doesn't want to live with that, with that reaction, with being forced to understand what's really happening in her head.

So she fights back, she tells herself that her experience with Sebastian is different, so different from her experiences until now with other men. Their close connection—she'd never experienced that… Without counting the feeling of déjà vu the first time she met him… Yes, she's convinced that a day will come when he'll admit what he felt too the first night. Katherine doesn't know any of that, she can't understand.

Except…

A vague memory comes back. The memory of an evening, when she went to a concert, he abruptly interrupted his conversation with another girl, also Indigenous, who he seemed very close to physically. For a moment, she felt a kind of envy deep down inside. Jealousy, yes. The girl was profoundly sexy. His type… And he was a respected artist, so it was normal that people wanted to talk to him, be close to him, touch him… Repelled by her own thoughts, she shook it off, pasted a smile on her face, and asked him if she could buy him a drink.

She resents Katherine for making her doubt; she's tempted to ask her to leave the apartment. It would be so much simpler…

"It doesn't matter, my friend," Katherine whispers, her tone less sharp, interrupting her thoughts. "I'm like that with my friends. You know, I didn't feel protected when I was younger. I did so many stupid things. And then I saw friends falling into the same traps. Getting into drugs, alcohol. I know you grew up in a town, but maybe it was small enough, out of the way enough, that you were protected from all that. I don't know…"

Monica takes a sip of coffee, weighs each word, but then she rouses herself from her own thoughts. What does Katherine know about her life? How dare she say something like that? But it's true, Monica had so little experience on the reserve… Her adolescence must have been nothing like teens in Kitigan Zibi, or in Toronto. Forestville! Monica isn't really even connected to what she should call her culture, while Katherine is a lot closer to hers, yes, and much more Indigenous than she is…

Monica holds her breath for two seconds. What did she just say to herself? Does she really believe that?

"It's okay, Monica. We can stop talking about it. I said what I wanted to say. Beyond that, it's up to you, but for real… Anyway, I'll stop. You can talk to me about it if you want. Come on, let's go sit in the living room, okay? I'm in worse shape than I thought, I have to say. I didn't sleep a lot in the end, ha ha! It was my party, after all. Oh, the Advil, here…"

She leaves the ibuprofen capsules on the table and stands up to go to the couch, her cup of coffee in her hand, and almost lies down, leaning on the couch arm, balancing her cup on her belly.

Monica follows her and sits in the little chair close to her unmade bed. The noonday light is streaming into the double room through the balcony door, forcing them to squint a bit. Katherine bends over and takes another sip from her cup but realizes she has already drunk almost all of it.

"Shit, I should have poured myself more hot coffee before flopping down. Now I don't feel like getting up again."

"I'd go, but I don't feel like it either!"

"Ha! It's okay, I'll get up again one of these days…"

Monica and Katherine giggle a little more, both with their noses in their cups, the tension between them finally dissolving into laughter. They did have a great time the night before, except for how it ended. The newness of their friendship heightens the feeling of having really enjoyed the party.

Monica is a bit calmer and lets her thoughts wander. "Katherine?"

"Huh?"

"Have I told you about my mother?"

"Not much, so far anyway."

Monica stares in front of her for an instant. She watches the tender green foliage outside moving in the breeze. For an instant, she again sees Sebastian standing there, smoking his cigarette on the balcony, and she pushes aside the image and the uneasiness that is trying to creep into her chest. The buzzing of the insects intensifies with each passing second, it seems to her, and time becomes fluid. Her mother. She wants Katherine to know her story, but...how to tell it?

Monica pulls a tiny thread so she can bring it to her lips and cut it with her teeth.

The pattern she's chosen is already beginning to take shape in the red glass beads. It was Katherine who got her beading again, showing her how one evening, after hours of watching Netflix together. She feels a lot less lonely since Katherine appeared in her life. They've become inseparable. Today, Monica is already halfway through the little personal project she started so she could relearn to sew and create using her people's traditional crafts.

Earlier that afternoon, she finished reading a novel. It had been a long time since she had read for pleasure, she'd been reading nothing but prescribed texts. This time, she treated herself to a book about a young mother's return to her village after leaving to give birth in Montreal. She consumed every page, one after the next until the end, so immersed in the story of a girl who was so much like her, in a way—not in terms of her experience, but in her way of seeing things.

The heroine of the novel had no father either. Monica's father had left when she was very young. It hadn't worked out between her mother and him. Johnny was his name. He left for another community, somewhere in Ontario, and never came back. Never contacted them again. She resented him sometimes, but at the same time, his absence didn't weigh very heavily on her. She was used to living without him. And besides, as a child she had all her grandparents, including his parents. At the time, she certainly didn't lack for love!

On the other hand, after the departure for Forestville, a distance developed. Then her grandparents died, one by one, during her adolescence. She often feels their absence, perhaps now more than ever. Alone in her apartment, for the first time since childhood, she is beading, thinking about what she has lost.

Monica loved her maternal grandmother, Émilie, best. She felt closest to her. But Émilie was the first to go. She got sick and died, too soon. She was fifty-eight. The image Monica has of her is the one in photos of the time in which she's wearing a skirt down to her knees, the classic white shirts that emphasized the line of her breasts, and her hair permed, which she was very proud of. Those were the glory days of curlers, and Innu women's hair is so thick and smooth that it took incredibly strong products to maintain the then-popular hairdo, the one like Queen Elizabeth II's. For Monica, Émilie was certainly a queen. A beauty queen. A queen of love.

"Miam ane, Nukem?"

"Ekuene! Bravo—tshe puketan!"

Monica wanted to be sure she had followed her grandmother's instructions. She could feel Émilie's benevolent presence looking over her shoulder, checking that she had gotten her sewing technique right. She congratulated her again to encourage her to persevere. Learning to sew takes a lot of time, precision, and patience, she had explained. It would take a lot for little Monica to be able to sew moccasins one day, for example. But at least she was learning.

The child slid another pink glass bead onto her needle

and pricked it into the piece of white leather that her kukum had given her as a pattern.

Émilie, who had set up her small sewing table in front of the window, gazed into the distance, toward the main street of Pessamit. She was lost in her contemplation—of the cars inching by, dogs wandering around the village in packs, teenagers laughing so loudly she could hear them through the window.

"Grand-maman?"

"Mmm…"

Émilie had glanced at Monica's small hand holding out her beading project. The fact that she had spoken to her in French irritated her a bit.

"Ekuene nituassim, miam en!"

"Nukem? C'est quand mushum e tekushet?"

"Apu tsissenteman nituassim, metuat natshiash tshia…"

Émilie smiled at her granddaughter, promising her once again that her grandfather would come soon, though she knew full well that her husband wouldn't be home before nightfall. If he came home at all.

The young grandmother started toward the kitchen to make tea. "Tshemen a nepishapui nituassim?"

"Eshe, grand-maman!"

She had watched from the kitchen while her granddaughter worked away. The girl was mixing the two languages, French and Innu-aimun, more and more, and Émilie was worried. She didn't want to see the language erased, so she had begun teaching it to young people in the village. Émilie was a respected seamstress in her community and told herself that one day Monica could also start making traditional clothes. She had worked in the village handicraft shop for a long time. She loved being surrounded by other women, other creators, gathering to produce cultural objects from another time. Perhaps by recreating them as faithfully as possible, they could give them value, Émilie said to herself as she sewed.

Monica's mother should have been about to join them. It had already been a few hours since she had left to make her rounds, visiting friends and family, and the afternoon had flown by… Émilie cherished the time alone with her granddaughter and used it to pass on what she cared about most: sewing and creation.

After filling the pot with water and turning on the stove, Émilie took a bottle of beer from the fridge and poured some into a glass on the counter. It was almost four o'clock. She took a sip, not thinking too much about her husband.

Distracted by returning memories, Monica hasn't noticed the knot in her thread, which broke when she gave a sharp little tug to get it through the leather. The beads she just strung are now scattered on the floor, to the delight of the cat, who bats them around with its paw, but Monica barely even feels disappointed. The start of her project doesn't look like much anyway, her stitches are too uneven. She can't refer to the original, since she didn't bring the little piece of leather to Montreal, its red, blue, and green threads sewn on a piece of hide that might still be intact, who knows. Material evidence of the bond between the girl and her grandmother. She could have used it, though. At twenty-seven, Monica hasn't sewn or beaded since her grandmother's death: she lost her teacher. The movements come back gradually, she just needs to—

There's a knock on the door. Cautiously, she gets up

from her desk, trying to avoid causing any more damage, since a single clumsy movement sends the glass beads flying everywhere.

"Good morning, madame, there's a package for you. Please sign here…"

Once the delivery slip is signed, in almost illegible cursive letters, looped together in a single line, and the mailman has left again after a quick *have a good day*, Monica closes the door. She's holding a small box wrapped in plastic with a shipping label on it.

There's no sender, no return address. But the handwriting is immediately recognizable. She has to open it in spite of the danger: anything in there will only reopen old wounds. She rips the plastic, tears off the label, opens the box, and digs under the crumpled newsprint, unhurried. She pulls out the buried object.

And there it is, in her hand. For real. The piece of white leather, with pink, yellow, and white beads sewn into the hide with thin red, blue, and green thread. She remembers the colours clearly. Lonely lines, barely straight, in one corner. Others that combine the work of the granddaughter and the work of her grandmother. In the leather, eras overlap, connect, join together.

The gigantic silhouette swirls in a cloudy grey sky, far too grey. Spreads its wings and hovers on the winds, up high.

Stuck on the ground, Monica trudges through sooty rain. Glimmers of brightness sometimes light up her footsteps, which show her exhaustion. She staggers. A single shout rings out in the air, and Monica stumbles over a small stone, crashing to the ground.

The winds pick up and she gets scared. Her heart beats faster.

The big black bird soars proudly high above, ignoring the drizzle, its shadow brushing over Monica.

She cries out to the bird: "You're not even worthy to call yourself Kakatshu!"

The winged creature doesn't seem to hear her calls. Monica is annoyed.

"Kakatshu isn't evil!"

The bird suddenly flies away. Monica watches the sky, waiting for the bird's return. Silence.

"It's not possible! It's no coincidence, that's for sure!" Katherine howls.

"Hey, chill out."

"But you told me it's been years since you spoke to her, and you didn't stay in touch. And then she sends this thing that's very important for you. Sorry, Monica, it's just that I find it absurd."

"No, no, it doesn't matter, Katherine. Besides, I don't really know if she was the one who sent it to me. But I mean, who else would have kept that? My mother! But as I said, it doesn't matter."

"If you say so. But you know what I think."

"Yeah, and I get that. The whole thing is a bit intense."

Monica serves her friend a cup of coffee. Slumped on Katherine's sofa, they both wake up after another nice evening of dancing, once again at l'Escalier. Monica thinks back to the night before. She danced salsa awkwardly with a guy named Étienne whom she'd met that day in the bookstore at the university co-op while she was with Gabriel, who was looking for books for his summer classes. She had already noticed the young man during an earlier night at l'Escalier. She often saw him there and found him attractive. Yesterday, she had had a chance to speak to him and spend the evening with him, so she gave herself a kick in the pants and did everything she could to make sure she got to dance with him.

But even so, she keeps glancing toward the entrance all evening. Disillusioned. Knowing that even if Sebastian made an appearance, Katherine would intervene. Which was for the better, no doubt.

Katherine's phone rings, interrupting her daydreaming. After checking the name on the screen, she answers on speaker.

"Hey, Gab! How are you doing? To what do I owe this morning call?"

"I need to talk to you about a thing for my Anthropology and Society course... Do you still have your notes from when you took it?"

"Oh boy, yes, I must have them somewhere... Do you want to come over? I'm here with Monica. Where did you disappear to at midnight, by the way? I thought you were going to stay out with us until the bitter end!"

"I told you I had a Tinder date! I was in too much of a hurry to say goodbye, you know," Gabriel guffaws.

"Hey, good for you! Get over here and tell us about it!"

"Okay, on my way!"

After an hour and a little commotion in the kitchen, Gabriel rings the bell as the two young women are finishing their scrambled eggs, fried potatoes, sliced avocado, and toast.

Katherine opens the door and Gabriel breezes in, exclaiming as he sits down at the table: "I really needed to see you!"

"Oh no! Was your date okay last night?"

"Yeah, no, the guy was nice and everything. But that's not what I want to talk to you about. So, I'm supposed to go to Vancouver next week for the Indigenous arts conference. But I also have to finish a twenty-page bibliography for the big anthropology paper I'm doing over the summer, and I completely forgot. Like, I've done nothing on it!"

"Well then, quit Tinder!"

"Ha! Yeah, it might be time to delete the app, especially since I think I've found the man of my dreams! No, actually, I was mostly short on time because I'm helping organize the Indigenous cultural evenings at l'Escalier. It's fun, but it's really time-consuming—the bookings, promotion, all that…along with everything else!"

"Admit it, you mostly want to stay because of your prince."

"Yes and no, I guess. I really have to finish my research…but I'll definitely take advantage of a few cuddles in the meantime! Ha ha!"

Monica watches the two of them teasing each other, captivated by Gabriel's laughter and his easygoing nature. In spite of the stress, the kind that would paralyze her, Gab manages to be completely present, enjoying the moment with his friend. The pressure to succeed at everything and the difficulty of managing her time are among Monica's own challenges, which sap her motivation and her interest. She likes to live in the moment. No pressure. She can feel the spiralling negativity that wants to swallow her up, especially when she thinks about school. Monica gives herself a shake and goes over to the coffee maker on the counter, which is still hot, to refill their cups, adding one for Gabriel, even though he already seems to be very much awake.

"And what would you like me to do to help, Gab, besides giving you my notes?" Katherine asks.

"Well, I was thinking about it, you know, and this morning it hit me... How would you like to fly to Vancouver to go to the conference for me? It's mostly the big collective exhibition of new artists I'm interested in. If you could go and see that, maybe one or two more galleries showing hot new artists, take notes, maybe a couple of little videos on your phone? That would help me a lot! There're going to be so many people at the lectures, nobody's going to notice if you don't go—but it's up to you, and it could be pretty good."

"What? You want me to go to Vancouver for you, that's what you're asking me to do?"

"Yeah! I'll just ask them to transfer the invitation to your name, it's InterNation that's covering the costs, and for their program the important thing is to send an Indigenous undergraduate student there. I've already checked, and it's fine with them."

Katherine opens her mouth but doesn't say a word. She looks back and forth between Gabriel and Monica, Monica and Gabriel, causing the two of them to laugh uncontrollably.

"Hey, Katherine, go for it!" Monica insists.

"Why don't you go, Monica. Actually, it would be your chance to see Vancouver."

"Me? But I don't know anything. I wouldn't know what to do, who to talk to."

"So go together, you'd just have to split the extra plane ticket."

The three of them burst into laughter again, but you can see in Katherine's eyes that she's no longer joking. She could rearrange a few things in her schedule, and in a few seconds gets excited at the idea of an impromptu trip. "I have an idea! Gab, you make the transfer to Monica's name. I'm just going to call my parents. They'll be able to advance me the money for the flight, and I can always take care of the rest."

It's Monica's turn to be speechless. Katherine's eyes are wide, and she gestures with her chin that Monica should say yes. She stands up, energized. "Come on! We totally have to go, Monica. Our first trip together! We'll go see the exhibits, the Squamish, Shuswap, Haida art, all of it. That'll give you all kinds of material for your newspaper columns! And Gabriel will be able to finish his stupid assignment and get it on with his new boyfriend! It all works out!"

"He's not my boyfriend yet! Let's not rush things!"

"Make sure he does become your boyfriend while we're off having fun in Vancouver!"

"Could you take care of my cat too?" Monica adds, getting caught up in the collective enthusiasm. "Otherwise I won't have anybody to check on her!"

"What's your kitty's name?"

"Well, it's Kitty…I wasn't very inspired. I call her that all the time anyway."

Raising an eyebrow, Gabriel laughs again and nods; she can depend on him. "You have to have fun and take notes too, okay? I'm counting on you, this'll be like the final touch on my work. And yes, I can take care of your kitty, darling! Oh, I'm so happy! Call me when you get there, we can even FaceTime from the exhibitions! Now go pack your bags, because you're leaving in three days. I'll email you everything once the transfer is done, Monica. Just send me your address and your student number, okay?"

"Wait a sec, it's really true? We're going to Vancouver?"

"Oh yeah! I'll take you to see one of the most beautiful cities in Canada, and you'll see, in that city, there are so many more Indigenous people and places and everything! I can't wait for you to see it! Woo-hoo!"

CHAPTER 3 *Vancouver*

The buildings flash by on either side of the road that leads directly from the airport in the outskirts to downtown Vancouver. Sitting beside her friend in the taxi to their hotel, Monica gazes at the skyscrapers and the sun shining through pure white clouds swollen with moisture, promising a good rain later that day. It's mid-July, and the first heat wave has already set in. It's still early. They left Montreal at dawn and went back in time, one time zone after the other, so that this day will seem supernaturally long. Fortunately, Monica followed Gabriel's advice, tacked on at the end of an email, and slept through part of the trip with the help of melatonin capsules she bought at the airport. She wants to make the most of every minute in Vancouver, doesn't want to be napping.

The road rises a little over one of the rivers that runs through the city, and the two young women enjoy a clear view of the high mountains rising in the distance north of the city, as the Pacific Ocean is unveiled on their left and their right, and countless tall green trees appear among the buildings and houses.

Katherine lets out a contented sigh. "God, I love Vancouver."

Monica turns to her friend, who is leaning back in the seat. She looks admiringly at her closed eyes and her smiling face. Coming back to this city seems to be good for her. Katherine told her about a lot of positive experiences she had here, and when she thinks of travelling, Vancouver is always one of her first choices.

Their taxi takes them along Howe Street, and when they arrive at the hotel, the driver helps the two women get their suitcases out of the trunk. Monica is distracted, fascinated by the huge skyscrapers and the hustle and bustle of the street. There's a couple in their forties at the corner, both Indigenous, a man and a woman. Dark skin, their heads held high; they are crossing the street talking, and soon a smile lights up the face of one, while the other bursts out laughing. Monica feels something so familiar in the passing scene…

The two travellers check in quickly and head up to the room, which, they discover, looks more like an apartment, with its corner kitchenette.

"Oh my god, do you see that, Monica? Gabriel didn't tell us he'd reserved such a big room. It would have almost been a waste if he'd come all alone!"

Monica puts down her bags and walks to the window, which extends from floor to ceiling. She slightly opens the curtains that protect the room from the blazing sun. "Wow! Kath, look at that!"

Katherine admires the exceptional view of the city. She can see herself again, in her early twenties, roaming the streets with her friends. The expeditions to Haida Gwaii, meetings with Indigenous students and with the chiefs of the region's different Nations. That was such a formative time for her, it helped forge her personality, her way of thinking and her vision.

"It's so beautiful, I can't get over it," Monica whispers.

"When I travel, I always imagine how places were

inhabited by peoples before. Here, they say the city is precisely at the intersection of the ancestral territories of three Coast Salish peoples: the Squamish, the Tsleil-Waututh, and the Musqueam."

"Yeah, and from way up here, it's really like that—you look at it and you want to imagine how it was before the concrete and all that... Do you think there are places where we could see, like, photos or paintings from before the city was built?"

Katherine sits down on the sofa and takes a few folded papers from her handbag. "I've got a map of downtown if you want. But yeah, we'll have to see, that should be possible. To start with," she says, holding up an index finger, "I have info on the exhibitions and the event tonight. We'll be able to ask there... We're just in time for the official opening of the conference. But before that, we really have to go to the Salmon n' Bannock Bistro. The food there is so good."

"Great! I'm just going to follow you. You're the one who knows the place!"

"Okay, grab your purse, and I'll give you the tour of my favourite spots."

Cross the Rockies and see only their peaks. Feel my body spread out and, just above the clouds, hold the wings of birds in my hands. The black shadow is the one who stole the sun. It steals it while I sleep, hides in the littlest box, sitting in a tiny cave between two mountains.

The chinook pushes us toward the starting place. We have to be worthy of our paths, the chosen itinerary. You have to earn every second.

Each downtown tower is a temple to the sky. Each window is a step to climb, tiers of the spirits.

A creature with its big wings spread, divided into sections of red, black, and the colour of varnished wood, cries out, wakes other beings made of the same. Everyone comes out of their hiding places among the crags of the Rockies. A great noise is heard. The clatter of the wood of their bodies. And a song begins. Even though their mouths are impassive, showing no sign that sound comes out of them, their voices join together to form a chorus that is impossible to understand but impossible not to listen to.

And the sky turns white.

Full of sun and bannock, Monica, holding her friend's hand, walks through the door and is surprised to see so many people at the opening of this exhibition of emerging artists from the Pacific Coast Nations.

The scene reminds her of the opening of the *Facing the Monumental* exhibit, except there's something so different here... But what? Suddenly it hits her. The other Belmore event showcased an internationally recognized Indigenous artist solely for the benefit of an almost completely homogeneous, almost entirely white, audience.

Here, there are white people from all walks of life, and their presence is no surprise, but they are not the majority in the modest main hall of the Bill Reid Gallery, named in honour of a great Haida artist. Katherine had told her the community was bigger out west, but that's not the only reason. There's a different feeling in the air, the impression that the possibilities for existing, for affirming one's art, are more numerous.

Monica is no longer even surprised anymore at the blend of strangeness and familiarity she feels and that seems to be a constant in her outings with Katherine, who is always quick to strike up a conversation, steering her friend from one group to another, as she recognizes faces from her time here during an exchange at the University of British Columbia.

The ceiling, infinitely high, is supported throughout the room by concrete pillars on which Monica recognizes paintings by a Tsimshian artist and video installations by another artist from the Squamish Nation, which she noticed when she looked through the documentation Gabriel gave them. After a while, wanting to immerse herself more completely in all the art around her, Monica decides to leave Katherine to her conversations, to the excitement of reconnecting with people, and heads off alone to a video installation. As she moves through the assembled crowd, the feeling of anonymity dissolves, and she takes the time to examine expressions and attitudes. She sees colourful personalities, clothes that express the sensibilities of Indigenous designers, others whose tattoos seem to represent ancient designs, possibly from cultural traditions of which Monica has no knowledge yet. There are proud faces, straight backs, bursts of laughter, which of course seem familiar.

The work that catches Monica's attention is designed to give the illusion that the viewer is in a canoe, paddling, experiencing the calm of nature, but also, according to the artist's description on the label next to the screen, reflecting on our relationship with the environment and the relationship our ancestors might have had paddling every day on the rivers of the land.

"Paddle. Love the river like you are marrying it. Never be afraid of the water."

I don't know how to swim, but I won't be afraid. Not afraid of getting in. Not afraid of picking up the paddle.

I will go forward. Even on the deepest lakes. The depths of which could swallow me up at any time, if they wanted to. If I wanted.

Monica feels a desire to thank the work, the artist who inspired that sudden yearning in her, the meaning of which escapes her, though its essential nature is obvious.

Why? Why has no one ever told me about this, about these possibilities, in my art classes?

Suddenly a bit dizzy, Monica takes a step to one side. She doesn't even have time to realize that she's stepping on someone's foot, and now she's bumped into that person with her whole body. Even their heads clunk together with a shock wave.

"Oh my God! I'm so sorry! Are you okay?"

"What?… Ah! Sorry. It's me…"

Monica searches for her words. Her limited command of English, acquired from a strange bird, seems to have evaporated completely. If only her memory could disappear so easily.

"I'm sorry, I…"

"C'est correct, je parle français! Except…it's been a long time, so I might have a bit of trouble…"

Monica looks at him, surprised. She notices his almond eyes, the irises that blend with the pupils. A whole world opens up in the darkness. The symmetrical tattoos on his arms catch her eye. Then there's his straight, pointed nose, high cheekbones, his bronze skin, his long black hair under a wide-brimmed hat of the same colour… The outfit vaguely makes him look like someone from the nineteenth century. His elegance intrigues Monica enormously. Who is this apparition, who moreover seems to speak good French, at least for someone on the West Coast?

"Mon nom c'est Oscar."

It's the beginning of an answer, but all her questions remain, they proliferate even, and soon she has millions, flitting around them, isolating them from the crowd. And yet she says nothing.

He smiles and holds out his hand to introduce himself formally. Monica, enthralled, doesn't know what to do with the attention.

"Je m'appelle Monica… They're really beautiful, your tattoos."

"Ah, merci…thank you! They're traditional."

Monica has an urge to look at them more closely, to ask the man displaying them their meaning, but the question is maybe too personal… She doesn't feel confident enough, and refrains. "Ah! Wow, fantastic!"

"Where do you live, Monica?"

"Me? I live in Montreal."

"Nice! Montreal is so cool. I love travelling there when I can. I hope you like Vancouver too." His voice is calm. He is composed, soothing, gentle.

"Yeah! I got here this morning. Vancouver is very nice. Yeah."

They both go shy, aware that their conversation is a bit too much like small talk, then they start laughing at the same time. Monica doesn't know what else to say. Could she look any stupider? But Oscar draws her out of her self-flagellation, offering his impressions of the canoeing video. Monica listens to him intently, but she's missing key aspects of what he says, getting only an occasional word. She's kicking herself for not having paid more attention in her English classes. Even an elective at an anglophone university in the city would have been useful…especially now!

Because of Oscar, but not just him. She feels a growing desire to make contact with English-speaking Indigenous people, mostly artists, to be able to learn more about the current situation and the history of the First Peoples of the west. Katherine had talked to her earlier about the major resistance movements in the region: the fight against the Burnaby Terminal, against Trans Mountain, among other things. She resolves to take more classes. She wanted to already, when she met the Raven. She tells herself, this time for sure, when she gets back, she'll get to it as soon as possible. Ah, Raven. Monica tries to push him out of her mind. She wants to forget him now. Take advantage of Vancouver to sever ties. That's really why she came. Katherine convinced her, in the end, without her really realizing it. She thought a lot about it, and remembered all the other nasty things about Sebastian... No, she didn't want to go through that anymore. She'd had enough of that when she was younger. She doesn't want it now. Oscar? He seems to be outside of all that, all those games. Oscar promises sincere feelings, authenticity.

A voice comes from the forest of timbers, amplified by a loudspeaker. Monica and Oscar turn their attention to a very small stage where artists are setting up a platform, barely a few centimetres high, just enough to raise the speakers a bit, so their faces can be seen clearly. Monica hadn't noticed that so many people had managed to find a spot in the gallery, which is now packed.

"I hope you're very proud of what we have today. Of course, we're thrilled to introduce to you these young artists who are destined to continue on the road of success, because their talent is phenomenal..."

The voice of the curator rings out in the gallery. His

remarks are followed by applause; there is a palpable excitement in the air and a huge smile on every face. Monica absorbs the sparkling energy like water from a stream. She sees Katherine in the crowd and watches her laugh uproariously with others, who seem to keep up with her friend's furious pace of conversation.

"Want a glass of wine?" a silky voice asks. It's the young man, whom she again discovers beside her.

She realizes she is bent over herself, her shoulders hunched, her chin tucked against her throat. Her head is bursting, she can't help comparing what she sees with what she has already known, what she's already experienced. Nothing in memory resembles what she has been suddenly immersed in.

She shakes it off and follows Oscar to the table with drinks and hors d'oeuvres. With a big smile, a woman serves them each a glass of white wine. Monica brings her glass to her lips, and that sip becomes for her the real kickoff of her stay in the big city of legendary British Columbia.

Oscar moves toward her, but just then a white woman comes over and lays a gentle hand on his arm.

"Mr. Wise, I got to see your work and I just wanted to let you know how amazing it is! Truly, you have so much talent, and you have to keep going! And…"

So he's an artist. Being shown here too. Monica moves to the side a little to let him receive his accolades. Oscar turns his head toward her while the woman prattles on, a one-sided conversation. He politely thanks the lady several times for the compliments. Monica's eyes meet his, and Oscar holds her gaze just long enough to make her heart beat faster. Yet the stranger's hand on his arm has managed to sow doubt in Monica's mind. She doesn't want anything unhealthy again. Is it just the woman's gesture, or is it an indication that Oscar could be…like Sebastian?

A little later, while Monica continues to move from paintings to sculptures and installations to charcoal sketches, Oscar goes up onstage and, to thunderous applause, brings both hands to his chest, smiling humbly. He bows to the audience to acknowledge the applause.

She does want to believe in it, in that encounter. Oscar is so luminous. Sebastian is darkness itself. She wants to ease her pain.

The room floods with stories she has never heard. The raven who steals the sun; giant canoes on the oceans; orca marriage guardians; invisible creatures populating the forests, making the trees tremble, called on for help as soon as bulldozers come to clear roads through ancient territories.

In Oscar's eyes, his eyes blacker than the beginning of the world, there are thousands of stars that want to speak of tomorrow.

But Monica finds Sebastian's pupils intruding in her mind, the infinite emptiness of his eyes. No planet orbiting any sun. And suddenly, the memory of Sebastian fades. She knew it, she feels it. She'd fallen into the hands of a lost, confused spirit who could so easily swallow her whole, take her vitality, feed on it. That's how he survives. And must have done with so many other girls, as Katherine told her.

There, in front of her, this new face is light, rivalling the light shining obliquely through the high windows of the art gallery. In the light of the day that is coming to an end, as night already whispers its promises of joy, laughter, and discoveries, the wrinkles on Oscar's face illustrate ordeals that have left their indelible mark. But they have not gotten the better of him: he is there, straight, in front of a seasoned crowd, triumphant, with talent and heart. He is accessible.

Several emerging artists, unknown or little-known—not known enough—are featured in this important exhibition. Monica has read the bios of each one, paying special attention to the Tlingit artist, who especially moved her. Oscar Wise is thirty-three. It seems clear that being here, for him, is an achievement, a major milestone. It seems clear that, yes, he welcomes with gratitude this gift of life, obtained at the cost of a long and laborious path for those who have come before.

Older than his years, Oscar Wise, with a gentleness that transcends memory, is the bearer of the wisdom suggested by his name, which has come across centuries of affliction, from a colonial history without mercy, without any respite for the original peoples.

When he comes back to her and asks in his laborious French which works are her favourites, Monica welcomes his presence. She feels calmer and continues to gain assurance as they chat, as he opens up to her, without reserve, without arrogance. He's trying, he says to her. He's making an effort. To do better, to embody what he dreams of for his people. And he knows he's at a turning point.

He is not Christ, oh no. He won't be the Messiah. It's just that he's reached an age when life settles into itself.

"When you can shelter behind your ramparts, a truce from clashes and battles, if that's what you want."

He says it to her, and she believes him.

"You have a choice. Continue in the war against yourself or seek the peace of your soul, to better continue the collective struggle of our people."

Redemption will be neither in heaven nor in hell. It will be on earth. On the lands returned to the original peoples.

Feeding the umbilical cord of perceptions, there is only the breath of the origin of our memory. Everything is dense, everything is throbbing. The world seems to emerge again, except that the heavens have not yet been born. Everything is black inside. In the belly of Earth, there is a beating. There is no heart. There is only a frequency.

What is it?

The children of the interferences running across the surface of the terrestrial bark. They are dancing. They are made of shadow and light. Of the charisma of sparks. Of the blood of the stars, light years travelled at the speed of silence.

Who are they?

The heavens. Broken into a multitude of atoms. Drops from the Milky Way. The walks of the bears, the martens, the geese. The course of spirits.

The sound. The sound of their feet on the wind. The invisible canoes carried on air currents. Together they are the song that rises softly from within our bones. Our bones resonate. Clatter.

Cracks.

Ants can raise cliffs. And the walls of my body fall. An avalanche of stones. The forests are carried off in the collapse with the deserts, the lakes, the watersheds. The insects penetrate each crack. Go down, come up again, populate. Others come into the world. Build mountains and, on the scale of grains of sand, a new civilization. Each in their turn, the creatures draw from my flesh to multiply. Everything is infinite.

The stars have a song. Each of them. One. There is not enough in one life to answer all the melodies the universe sings, whispers to us.

We are intermediaries. Something causes us to seek, to find, to link, to germinate, to express, to create.

Here, there is no conquest. No appropriation. No seizure. No looting.

Only the rising of a red sun.

"Your cat? She's a pain in the ass, but she's okay! I'm kidding! Kitty the kittycat gets anything she wants from me."

Gabriel, gesturing with his big hands on Monica's phone screen, laughs sardonically, while Monica smiles broadly, sitting in the back of a taxi.

"When are you going to talk to Katherine?"

"Well, you know...I don't really feel like it."

"Travel spats, classic. You kind of have to expect it!"

"Yeah, but it's not the same, Gab. We'll see when I get back, okay?"

Gabriel turns his attention to Monica's cat. Kitty is acting up and running all over the apartment. "Kitty, you're freaking out! You're making so much noise, you're going to bother the neighbours."

On the screen of his phone sitting on Monica's kitchen table, Gabriel sees the Mexican sun bathing his friend in shimmering gold.

Nestled in the back seat, holding her own phone to her face, Monica is watching the other taxis on the road, the impressive number of cars in front of them. From her point of view, there's mostly the grey of burning-hot asphalt... She sighs when she feels a breeze come through the lowered windows and touch her face. "Oh, wow! I thought it was hot in Vancouver, but Mexico is something else entirely. What about you, how's your work going?"

"Ha, lucky you! Don't rub it in. It's going okay, I'm getting there. I'm having trouble concentrating. Can you imagine if I'd gone out of town? If I were in Mexico, it would be a total free-for-all! It was a good thing you said yes to that crazy invitation, you know. For real, I feel good being in your apartment; it's quiet, there's no roommate... It works okay, even if there are no palm trees!"

"Anyway, thanks again, for, like, nudging me to go! I needed that so much..."

"It worked out for me too! But don't forget to send me your exhibition notes! And not just on Oscar, eh?"

Monica laughs in spite of herself. "I've got all kinds of stuff on the exhibition, on everyone, so there you go," she answers, suddenly bashful.

"Yeah, yeah! Okay, I'll let you get settled in, I'm going to make myself something to eat. We'll talk more later!"

"Okay, great! I'll send you my notes when I charge my phone, and my computer too. Love you! Hug my kitty for me!"

"Kitty says, 'Bye, leave me alone already, I'm busy with my new bestie!' Ha ha!"

"Okay, great! Bye!"

Gabriel blows a kiss to his phone screen before ending the video call.

Monica is alone with her thoughts. The taxi radio spews out ads in Spanish, which she can't understand at all. She'd love to be able to speak the language... Which reminds her of the promise she made to herself to take an English class as soon as she got back to Montreal, but instead she packed her bag and got on another plane. Oops! She could at least look on the Internet to see what will be available in the fall…but when will she have time, with university? That is, if she goes back. But yes, she will be going back, it's just…it's just that she doesn't know where she's at right now.

What she does know is that she was lucky to have a chance to go to Vancouver. She and Katherine met researchers from the Université du Québec à Chicoutimi who were affiliated with a university in Mexico and told them about a conference on Indigenous literatures of North America in Mexico City…the very next week! Once again, it hadn't taken much to organize, to plan departures, connections, all that. In fact, Monica cannot get over how much things have sped up for her since she met Katherine. Katherine, who's so far away now.

A song starts up, and she lets go of those stray thoughts. It's a typical song that makes you want to party, to dance on sultry evenings in the heat of the Mexican capital. Monica sighs. She doesn't know what awaits her, and maybe for the time being it's enough just to know that she's eager to find out. Latin trumpets blare boleros, like a prelude to wild adventures. Yes, she's in tune with what's happening around her. The blood is pounding in her veins like never before. What's happening? What's this road she's hurtling along, eyes half closed?

The FM radio starts up Luis Miguel's "La Incondicional." A ballad, a romantic song from what Monica can understand from the languorous music. She sees Oscar's eyes again, as if he were there, in front of her. She misses him.

They spent almost all their days and every evening together after the opening. They walked along the wharfs of the city. Found the beaches on the Pacific seashore. He took her to cafés and bars where Indigenous art was being featured or where artists from the various Nations of British Columbia were performing. She had been able to keep a certain distance from him and not throw herself into his arms right away, even though she had taken advantage of every single second. She had never experienced anything like it, and she was trying to follow her instincts: be careful with the relationship.

Late one night, when she got back to the hotel, she excitedly told a sleepy Katherine that Oscar had just introduced her to Zaccheus Jackson, an impressive Blackfoot slammer—he was outstanding, his words and his energy electrified audiences. Oscar didn't know him personally but had seen him perform many times, and just hearing Oscar talk about Jackson was thrilling. His friends and his fans were still mourning his premature death a few years earlier. Oscar and Monica spent hours watching excerpts from his slams on YouTube. Oscar, who described him as a major influence on his life and his art, showed her performances by people the slammer continues to inspire. Monica wanted to show some of those videos to Katherine, she was sure her friend would love them, but Katherine kept yawning, and her comments were completely unenthusiastic. They both went to bed shortly after, knocked out by the fatigue from their journey and all their encounters.

The taxi dropped Monica off in front of the Hotel Isabel, in the historic centre of Mexico City. When she made her reservation the day before, she had read that the hotel had the same design as the oldest houses in the neighbourhood, with distinctive colonial architecture bearing traces of the passage of time and peoples. She suddenly wonders if there are any hotels that feature the culture of the First Peoples of the region... She'll have to do some research.

After stopping at reception to get her key, she goes to her room, where huge vintage windows look out on the street. The wood window frames are solid, dark brown, varnished. Long white drapes hang from the ceiling to the floor, keeping the room at least relatively cool. In the street, Monica can hear the excited voices of tourists, the shouts of passersby, the calls of vendors, and especially the music blaring from all the businesses. She puts down her suitcase and jumps into the shower, luxuriating in the hot water and the fragrant foam. As soon as she closes her eyes, the coloured tiles are replaced with nighttime walks with Oscar, their meals in restaurants, the glasses of wine... He still fills her thoughts.

Shortly before she left, he told her he had strong feelings for her. Her first impulse was to surrender completely. Except something was growling inside her, demanding her attention. From afar. In a part of her being where all clarity was denied.

She's not sure what it is, but she noticed it as soon as she left Montreal. She ignored it for the first days. Then, with Oscar, the sound in her belly grew louder.

And now the growl is swelling. She knows she won't be able to silence it, but she chooses to muffle it with the noise of the crowd. After quickly drying off, then putting on a tank top and shorts, she tosses a few essentials into her purse and heads down the stairs, out of the hotel, and into the street.

At first she wanders aimlessly, just to stretch her legs and clear her head. Spanish is on almost every tongue around her, but she also hears English and even a few words of French on the sidewalks. Other languages too, foreign to her ear.

The historic centre of Mexico City is a tourist destination, certainly, but Monica has the impression of something stronger, as if she were in the heart of humanity. With close to ten million inhabitants, Mexico City is one of the largest cities on the planet. It is also unbelievably rich in history, and Monica feels immersed in it.

When she told him she intended to continue her journey all the way to Mexico, Oscar was almost even more thrilled than she was. Tenochtitlan, he told her, the city's traditional name, was already a metropolis of at least 200,000 inhabitants when the European colonists arrived, with the majestic capital of the Aztec empire, guardians of the noble pyramids of Teotihuacan, a few kilometres away. How was it possible no one had ever told her about this civilization in history classes during her schooling? She'd heard a lot about the American Revolutionary War, but she doesn't remember receiving the least bit of information on her other North American neighbour. She had to wait until she was almost thirty and able to travel to encounter that history first-hand, to discover that, still today, the Indigenous peoples of the region where she finds herself now, the descendants of the Mexicatl people, as they call themselves in Nahuatl, are helping to rekindle the spirituality of their ancestors and revitalizing the ancient ceremonies.

Oscar knows so much. But she is at peace with the fact that he is not physically with her. When she walks in the heart of the ciudad, he is with her in her thoughts, and that's just fine.

I have made my choice. Love was there, in front of me.

I was afraid, that's all. Afraid that it would amount to nothing in the end. Only illusion. Only a dream. Something fleeting. That it was just me. I who needed love so much. Who needed love so much.

But now I'm still hurting, I haven't been able to protect myself, even by fleeing, because his shadow is still with me.

The Raven is not dead.

I should stop calling him that... It's time, and I'm in the right place to leave all that here. Far enough away. A magical place.

I think I'm at peace with my choice to say no to Oscar. To tell him I need to find myself first. To say to him, "I think I can't love you."

She promised to let him know as soon as she got there. She'll do it when she gets back to the hotel, she thinks.

I'm sorry, Oscar. The journey awaits me.

In her pocket, her phone vibrates. It's a text from the head of the Canadian francophone delegation.

Hello, Monica! It's Stéphanie, from the conference group! Welcome to Mexico! We're glad to have you with us. I wanted to know if you got the schedule by email, otherwise I'll leave a copy at the reception of your hotel. I hope you have a lovely evening. We'll see each other tomorrow at nine! :)

Monica answers that everything is fine, that she got the information. She doesn't add that she hasn't yet looked at all the details, much less the schedule. She'll have to get up pretty early, she tells herself with a touch of regret, to take advantage of the breakfast included at the hotel. There isn't much wiggle room in her practically non-existent travel budget. Fortunately, Gabriel offered to pay part of the rent while he's holed up at her place to write.

She'll have to find a way to go to the pyramids. A way to escape, for just one day, from the rigid agenda of the conference. She has to go there and see those structures with her own eyes.

Oscar told her that in Mexico you can find the most ancient texts of Indigenous philosophies. She knows absolutely nothing about them but finds the idea enthralling. It was the first time she'd heard someone use the term *Indigenous philosophies.*

It drives me mad. I really know nothing at all about what I am. My childhood in Pessamit was so little, too little. And that stuff wasn't talked about back then… What's it like today? What do they talk about there?

I don't even know. I don't know what my village is like. It's crazy.

It's five o'clock. The city is teeming with life, still riding high on the afternoon, or gearing up for the evening, Monica isn't sure which. And it's only Wednesday. Fridays must be even livelier. But the conference begins tomorrow, and she has only five days here. Enough deliberation: she has to make the most of every moment.

First, she wants to familiarize herself a little more with the neighbourhood. Her GPS shows her that she can walk to the Zócalo, taking Calle 5 de Febrero, close by. On the faces of the Mexican women and men she meets, she recognizes features she was accustomed to encountering in Vancouver. Above all, they remind her of the people from back home. Like her aunt Marie-Anne.

Marie-Anne!

Yes, that woman looks like her, with her gentle face, though her eyes show worry… Monica barely remembers her aunt. Now here she is in front of her.

From memory to memory, she meets a gaze or a smile, reminders of her grandmother's neighbours. Her mother's friends. Some have no faces in her memories, and she can see only their hands, their feet. It was so long ago…

Monica stops for a moment to catch her breath. She feels a weight on her chest, but it's not only because of the infamous smog that regularly blankets the city. At a street corner farther on, she sees the giant flag of Mexico in the centre of the Zócalo. She's here. In the middle of the Mexican capital.

She picks up her pace, one foot in front of the other. Gradually something shifts, as if everything was becoming a bit fuzzy, the image vibrating. Reality is no longer tangible, it becomes malleable.

Bodies are duplicated. They proliferate. Ancient bodies, and bodies of today.

The eyes are the same.

Despite her sudden blurry vision, Monica decides to go straight to the centre of the square, close to the giant flag, like a lighthouse in the middle of this waking dream. Does she have heatstroke, is that why she feels off balance? She's afraid that if she asks for help she won't be able to explain what's happening to her.

Around her, people of all ages are walking past her, in all directions, hurrying. The square is full of those ancient memories, passing lives that have left remnants of their lineage, of their feelings, like a lingering aroma. Monica can see them all. There were joys, loves, flowers, and also sadness and despair. She takes it all in, from across the centuries. The gazes of the Elders. The women, the children. Their presence is strong. Unwavering.

Then a dark veil descends. Her eyes are still open, but

Monica has the impression that a delicate film is covering the surface of her eyeballs. She closes and reopens her eyes. The darkness fades, but her focus is slow to return. She stumbles, trips on a paving stone, and falls.

A stranger helps her up. The woman's hand grabs Monica's left arm and lifts her back onto her feet as if she weighed no more than a feather, or as if the woman were supernaturally strong. Monica blinks several times. Her vision recovers, and she looks at the woman who has jolted her out of her haze.

She is a woman whose features are marked by the years. She speaks to her in Spanish, her voice full of concern. Monica tries to gesture to her that everything is okay, nothing is broken, and the woman seems reassured, gives her her blessing and wishes her a safe journey or something like that. She walks off, another silhouette dressed in bright embroidered flowers among all the others.

Recovering her composure, Monica studies the crowd, trying to understand. Thousands of residents and tourists go about their business without paying attention to her, any more than to disappeared generations strolling among the multitude, trying to protect the places, to preserve the energy, maintain the balance, even between eras.

"What just happened to me?" she whispers to herself.

She rubs her forearms, the inside of her wrists, checking to see if she's hurt, and at the same time to clear her head.

Is this it?

Is she going crazy?

Monica, suddenly exhausted, decides to return to the hotel for the nap she should have taken after she got off the plane.

The nap turned into a full night of sleep, the deepest Monica had had in a long time. She got up at six and went to breakfast right away. Her awakening was a bit strange, with no dreams to ponder. She gulped down a delicious plate of huevos rancheros, the first in her life.

Now it's nine forty-five, and Monica yawns for the hundredth time in her uncomfortable chair. She turns to the table where the coffee is served and calculates her action before making her move. A speaker is presenting a PowerPoint in English on her research on Nahuatl. Monica tries to pay attention, but she's so tired she has trouble concentrating. The flight alone couldn't have been so exhausting. She thinks back to the feeling she had in her body yesterday, as well as her vision. Maybe that's it?

She stands up, the urge is too strong. There are about fifty attendees who have come to Mexico City to take part in this meeting of people from Canada and Mexico. Students, professors, and researchers are gathered in the inner courtyard of a magnificent yellow building. Monica walks behind all those people to go pour herself the coffee she's craving. She smiles at a Mexican woman with very brown skin and jet-black hair, then goes off to the side of the room, preferring to stand as she sips from her little cardboard cup of brown liquid while stretching her legs a bit. From her position, almost out of sight, Monica scans the diverse audience, then focuses on the group of women sitting in the front. She can make out only the profiles. Three of them, Indigenous Elders from Mexico, are listening carefully to a fourth woman, who is addressing the gathering. Monica understands that this woman is a researcher, also Indigenous, who is directing a project on local languages and their common roots with the northern Indigenous languages.

A young woman in the audience stands up and heads to the coffee table too. She has sun-kissed skin as well, and black curly hair, and she's wearing a long red summer dress. Monica feels a little envious. The only summer clothes she brought were tank tops and denim shorts, the basics she thought would be necessary here. The woman in red notices her and comes to stand beside her, cup in hand. Monica turns discreetly to greet her with a smile and a nod.

"I hope you're not too bored," the woman whispers to her in French.

Relieved to hear a language she speaks, Monica leans over to reply. "Don't worry, it's not too bad. It's like university classes, in fact. Just more interesting."

The young woman laughs, trying to make the least noise possible. She puts a hand over her mouth to hide her moment of inattention from the speakers. "I'm Maria Elena," she introduces herself in a whisper.

"Monica. Pleased to meet you. How come you speak French so well?"

"I did a year of linguistics at the Université du Québec à Chicoutimi, on an exchange."

"Oh, wow…and did you like the Saguenay?"

"Yeah, I loved it!"

"Hush!" One of the organizers comes over to let them know they're disrupting the session, even though they're speaking very softly. Her look says a lot about her character: it's better not to annoy her any further.

Maria Elena glances toward the doors leading to the busy street and, raising an eyebrow, invites Monica to follow her. Why not? The opportunity to learn more about daily life here is too good to pass up. Dropping their cups in a garbage can near the exit, they make their way outside, stepping into a quiet, shaded street.

"Here we can talk!" Maria Elena says as soon as the door is closed.

"Ha! Yeah. I guess I can take a little break, but I don't know if it's really good for me to leave…"

"Don't worry about it. I'm part of the team that helped organize the foreign delegation reception. The members saw me leave with you, so it's okay. Not to mention that you're the only Indigenous person from Canada among us. It's natural that I would want to take care of our guest."

"Oh, okay! I hadn't noticed that! It's great to see that on the schedule there are the names of the speakers and the names of their Nations, but I didn't realize about the Canadians…"

Maria Elena shrugs apologetically, then links arms with Monica and starts walking along the street, where a lot of tourists and local people are coming and going. It's a small cobblestone street, and colourful garlands hang high on the roofs. There are all kinds of craft shops, and street vendors, young and old, display handmade products or wave flowers for sale, presumably intended for the love of the buyer's life.

"I've often told them, though," Maria Elena continues, "that we needed to make more of an effort. Two years ago, we had five Indigenous guests from your country, but that's the most we've managed in recent years. You can't do Indigenous studies and have so-called meetings among Indigenous peoples if there aren't representatives from more than one or two regions! Our guests are mostly from here."

Monica laughs. "I understand. I don't know, though, maybe it's not really their fault."

"Don't you find that it shows how hierarchical education is in Canada? Anyway, that's what I think. It seems there are more white people in Indigenous studies than Indigenous people... Anyway, I know Stéphanie was really happy to be able to recruit you in Vancouver!"

Monica thinks for a moment about Maria Elena's point. Should she tell her she's actually studying art history? And Katherine, and Gabriel... But what she has just heard made her think: to a certain extent, she always knew there were imbalances, unfairness in opportunities, in access to education. She had never thought about the fact that something could be done about it. That something should be done about it. She tells herself that she will take more of an interest in the issue when she is back in Tio'tia:ke/Montreal.

"But I think it's going to change," Monica says. "I've just come from Vancouver. It was my first time there, but I attended the opening of an exhibition of emerging Indigenous artists and, there, we were in the majority. And mostly artists, to boot!"

"There you go! That's what I'd like to see! I think we've come pretty far. We've come...this far! It's time we came into our own, it's as simple as that."

"Maria Elena—that's right, isn't it? I like the way you think, Maria Elena!" Monica exclaims.

"Te digo, it seems to me, that's the very least we can do. Wait until I tell you my ideas for improving how the activities are organized at this kind of conference... More art, more culture! Less blah blah blah!" Maria Elena laughs.

Monica watches Maria Elena walking purposefully. It

is obvious that she is a strong-minded woman of ideas. The kind who makes things happen. Feeling more at ease, Monica decides to talk to her about her field of study, about her passion for Frida, but also for the works of lesser-known women, street artists, sculptors...

"Okay then, come on, I know where to go! I'll take you to see a friend. He lives very near here and, you'll see, his sculptures are incredible. He works with representations of Mixtec legends!"

Monica agrees to go along with the plan. The young Innu woman thinks for an instant about what prompted her to go to university. She chose to do the diploma in visual arts among all the options because she wasn't really interested in anything else when she started CEGEP. She didn't see herself working hard to succeed at math or science to get good grades. Good enough for what, anyway? And besides, her adolescence had been hard because of her relationship with her mother, and she had failed many exams over the years. She had good grades in French, geography, and history, and had still managed to graduate from high school. Going to college in Montreal was the best reason she'd found to get far away from home, so she registered at the Cégep du Vieux Montréal.

To her amazement, her growing interest in art history—especially because of one teacher who took her under her wing and initiated her in revolutionary artists—had pushed her to do whatever it took to finish her program so she could continue in that field. And that's what took her to her second year.

But by the end of the third semester, there was a void forming in her life. She struggled to focus on the subjects being covered, the books to be read, the assignments to be written. As the months went by, she lost interest in her classes. She dropped a few courses in her fourth semester early enough to avoid failing, and therefore was allowed to continue if she wanted, but just barely.

"Monica!"

Maria Elena's voice jolts Monica back to reality. Each time Monica revisits her memories or feelings of the last months, she feels dizzy. Maria Elena is here, she is calling her, she is beautiful in the light, tangible, warm. Real.

"He's here! Hola, Señor Hernandez…"

Monica follows her to the open front of a shop filled with colourful hats, fabrics of every hue, decorated with embroidered flowers or other patterns depicting mountains, pyramids, and roads criss-crossing the land. Mythic creations. Maria Elena goes in and kisses Señor Hernandez on the cheek.

"¿Que haces, Maria Elena? ¿No estabas a tu coloquio hoy?" Hernandez asks in a raspy voice.

"Ha ha! No, señor. Estoy con una mujer indígena de Canadá. Su nombre es Monica."

"Oh, hello! Monsieur…uh, Hernandez."

Monica greets him with a nod. She understood part of what Maria Elena said. Señor Hernandez points to a chair and she sits down. He is an impressive man whose stooped shoulders carry the weight of years of meticulous work in handicrafts. Physical work has made him a beautiful individual, luminous despite his sober appearance.

The sun that blankets the whole city extends its glow into the shop, illuminating their faces. Hernandez speaks again in Spanish to Maria Elena, looking at her with his dark eyes.

"Hernandez wishes you welcome here and he says he's happy to meet you, Monica."

"Ah, moi aussi, monsieur!" Monica answers, bowing

slightly to their host. "It's an honour for me to be received by an Elder of the community..."

Maria Elena translates for Hernandez. The man again speaks to the young Mexican woman in Spanish.

"He says he'll be taking part in a ceremony in two days. This Saturday, in fact." Maria Elena smiles mysteriously. "I'm glad to know there's going to be one this weekend."

"Oh yeah? What kind of ceremony?"

"A peyotl ceremony. It's a privilege to be invited, you know. Señor Hernandez is one of the men and women who now teach those rites to others. Especially young people our age. He's inviting us both. Are you interested?"

"What's peyotl?"

"I can't tell you more for now, because you'll see there, but basically, it's a cactus with no spines. It's always been used as a guide to receive visions and messages from the invisible world."

"Ooh...wow! I'm really impressed. Thank you! It's so nice of you to invite me, especially since I'm a stranger!"

"It's nothing. You'll be able to have a real experience of the country, a connection with the ancestors. Besides, you're not a stranger. We're Indigenous people, we're all connected with each other on both continents of the Americas. We're brothers and sisters."

"You know, I've never experienced a ceremony before, not even back home. So here...this is going to be really special. You'll be there too?"

"Yes, I'll go with you."

Monica is reassured by her new friend, who promises to provide her with sympathetic guidance. Maria Elena repeats that Hernandez is a generous man, the keeper of a great deal of spiritual and ancestral knowledge, and Monica feels that something important is about to happen in her life. Concluding the agreement with a smile, Señor Hernandez shows the two women through his studio, giving Monica a chance to discover his art, which already offers her access not only to his history and his ancestors, but also to his present and his hopes.

That evening, after the conference, several of the participants who already knew each other, women in their twenties and thirties, including Monica and her new friend, gather at the Pakaly Bar, on a pedestrian street lined with restaurants and bars, a couple of blocks from the Hotel Isabel.

The evening goes by in a spirit of friendship, with laughter, drinking, and sharing stories from each other's countries. The sense of humour of the Indigenous peoples of the south is just as sharp as in the north, Monica thinks several times. It's maybe even more absurd. She feels understood; these new friends can read her like an open book. The boisterous laughter mixes seamlessly with the lively noises from the street as the hours pass.

It all makes Monica acutely aware of the absence of Katherine. Katherine, who so quickly became her best friend. She would have liked to share this moment with her.

Between two sips of beer, Monica recalls their dreadful argument in the hotel room in Vancouver. It was the last day of their stay. They had celebrated the end of the trip and the invitation Monica had just received after a panel where she had spoken a few times, which would have her head to Mexico almost immediately after their return to Québec. They had toasted the Monica World Tour with round after round of shooters.

When the two returned to their hotel room, Katherine was drunk, in a state of really advanced intoxication. Oscar, who had spent the evening with them and wanted to make sure they were safe, had insisted on going with them. As the elevator was taking them back to the studio suite, Katherine, propped up on one side by Monica and on the other by Oscar, had started talking about Sebastian, her words muddled. She seemed to have forgotten what Monica had confided in her about her magical experience with the West Coast young artist over the past few days. The timing was particularly bad because that very morning, Monica had explained to him that she needed time, that she did not feel available for a relationship right away.

Revisiting the past with Sebastian, Katherine peppered her rambling story with criticisms of her friend, pointing out her mistakes, how easily she let herself get taken in. Embarrassed, Monica had tried to answer her just as harshly to let her know that this was not the time to dredge up the past. She didn't want Oscar to imagine that Sebastian was still in the picture, or that she could have had such an unhealthy relationship with someone. This was not the first time that Katherine had revealed to others painful details that Monica had entrusted her with. But this time, the drunken outpouring had been deeply humiliating, especially since Katherine had herself spent the evening with the friend of a friend, a certain Dave with whom she had had a bad experience years before. Monica didn't know the whole story, but it was clearly a bad idea. She only knew that under the effect of alcohol Katherine had let Dave get close to her and flirt with her all evening. If she had been thinking clearly, Monica would have quickly realized that Katherine had rehashed her past to avoid dealing with her own guilt about falling into old patterns.

Monica was so hurt that she hadn't even noticed that Oscar—magnificent, magical Oscar—had been understanding, not commenting, wanting only to make sure Katherine and Monica got back to their room safely.

He left quietly, wishing Monica good night and closing the hotel room door behind him. Turning to Katherine, who had slid down to the floor and was lying on her back, Monica poured out her wrath.

"Why did you talk about Sebastian? That guy is dead to me! I learned my lesson, you told me yourself, you predicted that I would regret my feelings for him. Okay, fine! It's over! But why did you have to say all that in front of Oscar? Why did you talk about me like I was a fool, a slut, some stupid girl, in front of him? Shit, Kath!"

On the road to the airport, they hardly said a word to each other. They parted at the Montreal airport without even saying goodbye, taking separate taxis home. Monica's annoyance subsided a bit when she finally recounted the fight to Gab—it hadn't taken much to convince him to stay a bit longer to hold the fort and look after her cat—but not enough to contact Katherine before leaving for Mexico three days later.

But this evening, savouring this beautiful grand night in Mexico City, with its freight of so many centuries and so much resistance, she misses her best friend so much. She knows that living this euphoric moment with her, her fellow adventurer, would have made the experience even more amazing. She would call her. They had to talk.

The evening ends shortly after that melancholy

moment and she feels emotional again walking toward the hotel with Marie Elena, along the street still full of tourists drawing out the party. Arm in arm, they never stop laughing. Both of them nearly stumble and fall, giggling non-stop.

Monica, since the beginning, since the first words whispered in her ear, had felt attracted to Maria Elena. She doesn't know how to tell her, she's not sure the feeling is mutual. Throughout the evening, she pushed aside the idea of taking a chance and inviting Maria Elena to sleep with her. Maria Elena has a sense of humour, and Monica has fun with her, she loves to laugh with her and talk about all kinds of political issues. Several times, though, Monica has felt connected to her, in a particularly intense way. She could almost feel sparks fly. Her intellect, her opinions, and her way of expressing them make her so beautiful, sexy, desirable, that Monica's crush on her has only intensified over the course of the evening, until Maria Elena seems completely irresistible.

And now, to her great surprise, she's here, at the end of the evening, walking arm in arm with her and laughing. With Marie Elena, in the streets of Mexico City.

At the hotel, Monica climbs the stairs to her room, Maria Elena still holding her hand, looking deep into her eyes. She turns to wish her good night, but with that look, Monica understands.

In the room, their bodies entwine. Yes, there was a mutual desire, a strong attraction, fed by their instantaneous connection, after a day spent together sharing laughter and knowledge.

When Maria Elena puts her lips on Monica's, the kiss lights a fire in the middle of the room. A burning human heat. Under Monica's eager caresses, Maria Elena's body quakes and quivers; then, covering Monica's body with kisses, she silently prays for the constellations to descend to Earth to wrap them both in their firmament.

Maria Elena is sitting beside Monica in the back seat, leaning against the door and gazing out the window, even though it's dark out. Glancing out on her side to see what has caught Maria Elena's attention, Monica sees that the sky is clear, the stars shining brightly.

The conference lasted only two days, but Monica's flight, like those of the other foreign participants, is scheduled for Sunday. The attendees were given all day Saturday to visit the exhibitions in the city, with Sunday for their return.

On Friday, the joyful mood made up for the fatigue, and Monica was able to recover enough to attend plenary sessions during the day, since she had agreed to give Gabriel a report, as they like to call their overly detailed documents—he was impressed by what she told him about the events she attended in Vancouver. *It's as if I was there. Even better, because I never take good notes!* She also intends to put together the information she needs to write an article for the UQAM newspaper, in which she wants to suggest regular collaboration on Indigenous art around the world. One more reason to keep hanging out in her department…

Once the conference was over, Monica allowed herself a solid twelve hours of sleep. The next afternoon, the two women left Mexico City, heading to the ceremony site.

For about forty minutes now, they have been riding in a car, with a man and his wife sitting in front, following another car carrying Señor Hernandez. Monica knows that the ceremony will be held in Valle de Bravo, an hour and a half from the big city of Toluca, where Maria Elena's family lives. After travelling from Mexico City by bus, they stopped to have a bite at Maria Elena's parents' house before joining the cars the rest of the way.

The excursion gives Monica a chance to discover a bit of what's beyond Mexico City and to taste the various specialities of the peoples of Mexico along the way. She learns that Maria Elena is half Otomí through her mother, and that the young woman is part of a youth movement in her region, calling for the rehabilitation and revival of ancient rites and traditional knowledge that have almost been lost, largely through the imposition of the Catholic religion, which is very strong here.

During the last part of the journey, a few shooting stars appear in the sky, leading to conversations about heavenly bodies, constellations, and space.

Soon Monica notices other lights closer to the ground, even more striking. The blue lights sparkling in the distance in the huge fields extending behind the farms, someone whispers, are the work of little beings of the forests and fields that light up the night to illuminate their gatherings, their dances. When they are shining, you mustn't go anywhere near for fear of making them disappear as a punishment for your presence. Monica knows she will never forget.

They're in a place she would never be able to find on a map. There's no signal, so she wouldn't be able to find it with her GPS either. Monica meets a large group of Indigenous women, some from the southern United States, and others identifying with various peoples of the big family of the Nahuas.

These women have all come to take part in the peyotl

ceremony. Maria Elena, respectful of every detail of what has to be done at the ceremony site, shows a touching level of devotion for the man who will guide them, and especially for the women Elders present there. They are received in the big courtyard of someone's house, and the sky is huge and clear. Since the village is at a high altitude, it feels like you can touch the heavens.

Maria Elena introduces Monica to everyone. Light-headed from the dance among the shadows, Monica is sure she won't be able to remember everyone's name but tries as best she can to memorize the faces, the eyes. Again and again, she is welcomed. Maria Elena provides translation, conveying among other things that they are happy to have a visit from an Indigenous woman from the north.

Monica becomes gradually aware of the solemnity of the moment. She's a bit disoriented, afraid of not being worthy of her place here. Then something dawns on her. She was invited, she is welcome, she simply has to take advantage of what is being offered, surrounded by Indigenous women of all ages, in the heart of Mexico, in the middle of the night, all of them watched over by the sparkling firmament.

The ceremony is going to begin; they have to take their places. And Monica, suddenly, feels inside something that fills her until it warms the surface of her skin. A dull growl rises in her chest. She places her two hands on her torso. She prays that the plant, the peyotl, will let her to see what she's supposed to see.

Already, she feels incredibly grateful for this journey, beside Maria Elena, in a world that she recognizes more and more with her soul.

*I have seen
the Pleiades.
Up close.*

In front of her, on a large expanse of sand, a beach she does not recognize, stand dozens of Indigenous women, Elders from all the Nations of the Earth.

Each one is staring at Monica with her black eyes.
A flight of geese crosses the sky above them.
Monica does not know what to say to these women.
She has never seen them.
And suddenly, a great silence descends.
It is enough.

Throughout her whole body, Monica suddenly feels filled with love.

Return.
I have to go back. I can't go on without knowing my
home. My country is the North Shore. Nitassinan, I know
your name, you know mine.
Nitassinan.
Nutshimit.
Nitassi.
My land.
Home.

I am at home everywhere in the Americas. Everywhere
I go, our people have been present. Our languages have
been present. Our cultures have been celebrated for
centuries.

I have to relearn to call home the land that saw my birth.
Return to the village of my childhood. The village of my
mother and my grandmother. Know my family again.
Recognize the faces of my people.
Return home. If I don't, I can't move forward.

No return.
I don't understand why I don't know my home.
Who drove me away?

Return.

The enormity of feeling alone.
Everything surrounds me, touches me, sweeps through my
hair on a gust of wind.
My heart beats slower in the hot, heavy air.
A liquid envelops me.
When I breathe, little bubbles escape from my lips.
Have I drowned?
I hear words spoken to me but understand nothing.
A thousand hearts are beating in my head, a dull
knocking.
The dawn becomes clearer, calls me back, brings me back
from the shadows.

No return.

I don't know my home.

It was my mother who never wanted me to go back.

She took me away as if I was never supposed to live there.

I couldn't belong there. But she is also a daughter of Pessamit, just like her mother.

The only thing I want to say, the only meaning I can find, is that it's surely my mother and my grandmother's fault. Now I have to live with the consequences of their actions, the choices they made during their lives. I can't call myself Innu. Can't feel I belong to my village.

I have never wanted such a wavering spirit, to be so innocent, to fall prey to people who want to take advantage of me, of my strengths and weaknesses. I have chosen nothing of all this.

I want to heal. But…

It's not up to me to heal everyone.

It's not up to me to carry the weight of the people who came before me.

I decide to leave the house and head down the sandy slope where the cars are parked, and I cross Kesseu Street to take the path that runs past the house across from ours.

Along that trail, the trees are gigantic. The leaves are soaked and shine lush green under the July sun of the Innu summer. The mosquitoes are dancing, and other big insects swirl around, frightening me. Their wings hum and I keep walking, past the convenience store and the sign announcing that the proprietor's name is Florence.

I cross another street without slowing down, and I come to the little white house. I can barely climb the wooden stairs. The door is wide open to visitors, and the windows are full of brown plastic dolls, leather shoes, and tanned leather coats with hand-embroidered flowers.

No one pays attention to me, a five-year-old girl walking behind the display cases and through the doorway with its hanging strips of leather decorated by multicoloured beads. There are all kinds of Innu women busy with moccasins, dolls, leather clothing. Under the fluorescent lights, they are embroidering patterns, pushing shiny needles through the hides. I'm looking for my grandmother.

"Kukum!"

The women start laughing. Their voices get louder, and a new wave of laughter sweeps through the room. I run past them, between their work tables. My grandmother comes in through the back door, which is also wide open, in the late afternoon light when the sun turns orange, wrapping the village in its warmth, just before the evening refreshes us. Outside, to one side, women are smoking their cigarettes, taking a well-deserved break.

"Tshekuan tuman uteshen! Tanite ma tat tshekaui!"

What am I doing here?

"Tshidapedem la télé nekaui..."

My mother is watching television at home. She thought I was playing quietly with my toys, but I left the house and ran to the shop.

My kukum sits back down in her chair and takes me on her lap to show me what she's working on. It is the upper of a moccasin, which she is decorating with a symmetrical white-and-mauve flower.

She takes my little hands in hers and slips a thimble onto my index finger. She helps me place it on the end of the needle, which pierces the leather, pushing my finger with hers. I'm sewing! Her hands, browned by the sun, wrap around mine, dirty from the sand in the yard.

"Ekuene nituassim!"

That's it, my child. You push the needle into the leather, it goes through to stitch the purple thread, and then it will cross time and space. And we'll be there on the other side. Some say that will be the end. In truth, it will be the beginning.

Monica undoes her seat belt as the car rolls down the slope on Ashini, the street that brings you into the village. She presses the button to open the window on the passenger side. The breeze comes in, cool. Monica closes her eyes. Her hair is dancing.

She smells the fragrance of the fir trees and breathes in the aroma of the Saint Lawrence River. She shivers.

Katherine, back at the wheel after the last fill-up, watches her friend out of the corner of her eye. She smiles, glancing at the trees, the big hill that overlooks the first houses coming up on the left. On the right are the police station and the fire station. The Pessamit convenience store.

"You can continue to the end of the street, and you'll see the Saint Lawrence. I'd like to stop there first," Monica murmurs to her best friend, opening her eyes.

Katherine nods without speaking. The smile fluttering on her lips seems to say everything.

"There's my grandmother's house. Where I grew up, before Forestville."

Monica points to the right, and Katherine gets a brief glimpse of the white-and-royal-blue house. Sturdy trees with little red berries honour the house with their beauty. Driving very slowly, not going over the regulation thirty kilometres an hour, they continue on their way.

"How are you feeling?" Katherine speaks very softly to Monica, as if she doesn't want to disturb her friend's homecoming.

Monica looks at the passersby, who in turn gaze at the car and its occupants. Each house reminds her of something. A person, a moment from childhood, when she walked in the streets with other children. Of course, she doesn't remember their faces anymore. "I feel good. For now."

Monica had no trouble convincing Katherine to go

with her to Pessamit. Before leaving Mexico City, she was already planning to make the trip, only she didn't know right away when exactly she would be able to follow through, or if she was really ready. Maybe there would be so much she needed to clarify before going that the return would be perpetually postponed. Finally, after a few suffocating weeks in the mugginess of the Montreal summer, working on a few articles about various Indigenous artists in Vancouver whose work she had really enjoyed, and other writing that was a little more for herself, and also exchanging a few emails with Oscar, the inner call came, and it was a lot stronger than anything she could have imagined. From that moment on, everything quickly fell into place.

The car, borrowed from Katherine's mother, who had left on her annual Sun Dance circuit and was happy to encourage her daughter to discover the North Shore, rolls on as far as the presbytery and the church beside it, both facing the Saint Lawrence. The young women gaze at the windswept, decades-old church on the coast. Looking farther to her right, Monica notices two families with three young kids coming out of the health centre, walking fast, looking happy. The people are smiling. Every person they've encountered since arriving was smiling or laughing heartily in the summer sun.

After stopping at the intersection next to the presbytery, they cross Laletaut Street, and Katherine parks on the other side, on a patch of gravel across from the expanse of water. In front of them, a steep slope leads down to grass, tidal flats, and the sand beach.

"This is it, this is your home. What do you want to do?" Katherine asks, stepping out of the car to get a breath of fresh air off the Saint Lawrence. Monica decides to do the same thing.

"I feel like taking a walk on the beach. How about you?"

"Yes, I've been anxious to see the beach ever since Gabriel raved about it. The weather's so nice too."

Monica turns toward the beach, where she doesn't see anyone. Despite the beautiful weather, they will have the beach to themselves.

Going down the sand road, which turns into a path winding through the grass, they come to the shore. The place is peaceful, in spite of a few cars passing on Laletaut Street and the sound of children in the distance. When they come to the edge of the water, everything has gone calm, everything has slowed down, and a silence filled with the white noise of the waves takes hold. The breeze joins in, starting to sing in the quiet.

Here, the path goes either to the right or the left, following the shore that runs along the village and where all the streets end.

A vague memory comes back to Monica and prompts her to head west. In that direction, the sand runs along Metsheteu Street, which has the same name as the bay where it ends, at the estuary where the Betsiamites River flows into the Saint Lawrence.

The two women walk in silence, Katherine following Monica. As they go on, the wind seems to get stronger, making its presence felt. The beach extends in front of them, seemingly to infinity. Monica walks very close to the water, where the waves fall, rubbing up against the shore. She stops for an instant to take off her shoes, carrying them in one hand. Seeing her, Katherine decides to do the same thing, walking a little deeper in the waves.

Soon no noises from the village reach them. From the Saint Lawrence either.

Monica stops suddenly.

"Are you okay, Monica?"

"Didn't you hear it?"

Monica turns around and glances at Katherine, who, perplexed, asks her again: "What?"

Monica looks around.

"Monica?"

A new silence, a time for listening to surroundings. Katherine could swear there's nothing but the song of the wind and the dance of the waves.

"I heard someone walking, really close to us."

Katherine, a bit uneasy, doesn't know what to say. "Well, maybe it was me who—"

Monica again turns to her friend. "I know where you are, where the splashing is coming from. What I just heard came from over there." Monica points to a spot a few metres away.

Katherine doesn't dare take another step. She fingers the hem of her shorts. "I've really always been afraid of those things…"

"What?"

"I'm afraid of those things. The…the spirits, you know."

"But you do ceremonies, come on! Since you were little!" Monica holds back a laugh.

Katherine says, "Yes, but it's not the same. In the ceremonies there's a structure. Outside them, there's nothing!"

"I get it. But I swear I heard something that didn't come from us. It was a bit strange…"

"Don't say that!"

Monica can't stop laughing. Katherine's voice has just gone shrill in a way Monica has never heard.

Katherine, seeing her friend's reaction, laughs shyly in turn. "I swear, Monica, you shouldn't tell me crazy things like that."

"But it's nothing, Katherine! It's nothing. It's just…"

Katherine sighs and laughs, then starts to walk again, her stride more determined. "Hurry up, let's go to the end of the beach before I decide to run away!"

Monica tries to match her friend's quick pace, but walking in the sand is difficult, and she keeps laughing as she stumbles behind Katherine, who refuses to slow down, throwing up a spray of water as she walks, which makes the situation even funnier.

"Stop laughing at me!" Katherine cries with a little smile.

Monica drops to her knees in the sand. She can't help herself anymore.

Katherine turns to her and laughs in turn. "Go on, get up, we have to go see your aunt soon, you can't stay here forever!"

Gasping with laughter, Monica can barely answer between two hiccups. "Wait…I need to…to laugh some more!"

Katherine kneels down in the sand too, and they both give in to their impossible longing for quiet.

"How can I say this? You'll notice, with time, that things like that always happen in the communities," Katherine explains back in the car.

"What are you talking about exactly?"

"I don't know what to call it… Supernatural things? No, what I mean is, it's not the same with us. In the sense that I really believe there's an invisible world and it often manifests. In the time of our ancestors, it was just…always there. And now, I find, when we go back home, we often hear stories that white people would call supernatural. For us, well, I think it's normal. You know, like the time with the invisible bee, when we talked about ceremonies, after the exhibition? That's what it is. I think we stayed connected to all that, and when we forget, the spirits appear. Anyway, I'm trying to explain simply, I hope you understand, ha!"

"Yeah, Kath, I think I know what you're talking about… But the sound of footsteps, just before, was that to welcome us, or what?"

Katherine turns and winks at her with a laugh. "Could be. I thought of that too. I'm afraid of those things, you know, but I thought the same thing."

"One day you'll explain it to me, Katherine Shetush! How can you be a rebel and at the same time such a scaredy-cat?"

"Sure! But don't say anything about this to Gab or Justin, okay?" Katherine pulls into the unpaved spot in front of a burgundy house. She barely has time to turn off the motor, take out the keys, and get out of the car, and Monica is already at the front door. She knocks, then opens without waiting for an answer, as things are usually done around there.

Katherine starts to follow but stops suddenly. Monica glances back at her friend, surprised she's not coming, but Katherine, with a conspiratorial, friendly grin, motions to her that she'll wait outside. Monica goes through the door alone.

Katherine heads back to the car and leans against the hood to contemplate the surroundings. On the road, her co-pilot talked about this street, Pisto Street.

Katherine gazes off toward the horizon, her face caressed by the wind. The late-afternoon sun is nestled behind the clouds. Over the years, she has met lots of people from Pessamit, who were either passing through Montreal or had come to the city years before. She's long heard about this place on the shore of the Saint Lawrence but never had a chance to visit. She appreciates this moment all the more because it's been such a long time coming. She's heard so much about the sunsets, the wind on the river, long days on the beach, and fires in the evening. And the colour of the sky at different times of day, about the comforting breezes and the smells of the forest all around, unlike anywhere else. They weren't exaggerating.

Inside, Monica doesn't find anyone at first. She calls the name of the woman she hopes to find here, her last connection to the village. "Marie-Anne?"

She starts to feel a bit worried. It never occurred to her that her aunt might have left. In that case, who could she turn to here? There is not a sound in the two-storey house. Standing in the doorway, a bit lost, Monica glances at the basement stairs, then peers into the darkness at the bottom.

It has been fifteen years since she has been in this house.

After a moment that seems endless, a rather short woman appears, dragging her feet. She looks half-asleep, her arms crossed, pulling her light green sweater around her.

"Kuei?"

The woman is simultaneously trying to open her eyes and squinting to see better.

"Kuei... I'm looking for Marie-Anne. My name is Monica. I've come from Montreal. I'm Claire's daughter."

Marie-Anne's face—it is her, Monica recognizes her when her features brighten—suddenly breaks into a big smile.

"What? Monica? My niece!"

Trotting quickly to her kitchen, the old lady calls to Monica to come and sit down at the table, then busies herself making tea. She turns on a burner to maximum and grabs her metal teakettle to fill it with water from the faucet. Monica takes off her shoes at the front door.

"What are you doing here, dear? When did you get here?"

"Just now...I just arrived. About two o'clock," she answers as she sits down at the table.

"Well, well! My goodness! I'm so happy to see you. This is a real treat!"

Marie-Anne goes over to Monica and gives her a hug. The long embrace of a reunion, in silence. At first, Monica doesn't know how to respond to the gesture. Marie-Anne's warm greeting catches her off guard, but she finally surrenders.

With the teakettle on the stove, Marie-Anne comes and sits down at the table across from her niece. She looks up, and her eyes meet Monica's, and she gives her another disarming smile. Monica vaguely remembers the interior of the house. She was just a child the last time she was here.

Outside, Katherine starts the engine. Before backing out, she grabs her phone and texts Monica, just to let her know.

I'm going for a drive, take your time xx

She pulls out of the parking spot and heads toward the beach.

"It's been a long time…since I've come back here."

Marie-Anne looks soulfully into Monica's eyes. Until now, Monica has avoided her gaze, but now she can't break free. It's hard to deny, despite her calm, simple ways, that Marie-Anne is a bit intimidating. She does seem sincere.

"Your mother's my little sister, you know. It's been a really long time since I've seen her too. I haven't heard from her in so many years!"

Marie-Anne speaks slowly in Innu, pronouncing each word separately. The village accent brings back all kinds of childhood memories for Monica. She realizes she didn't know she was so attached to her memories. That she could remember so much. Especially the moments shared with her grandmother Émilie. The voices, the smells. On the other hand, she can't recall the words, though she knows that she lived then almost entirely in Innu-aimun.

"Is this the first time you've been back here?"

"Yes…it's the first time. I thought I was going to… It was to…" Monica doesn't know how to find the words.

Yes, how? Yes, why? Did I have the right to come back here? Do I have the right to stay?

Suddenly, all these questions are scrambled in her mind.

"Yeah, well, what is it you're looking for, after all this time?"

Can I belong to this village? Can I be at home here?

"I wanted to see you again, basically…I wanted to see you. And I'd like to find where Grandma lived. I mean, where she lived when she was going into the woods. And her grave maybe? I don't know…"

"Oh, Monica! I'm happy to see you," Marie-Anne exclaims again, as if she can hardly believe her niece is sitting in front of her. "You're so beautiful. So tall! You've become a woman! We'll take the time to talk about all that together. But first I want to know, are you in school?"

"Yes. Well, I'm trying to be. I'm doing a BA in art history, at UQAM."

"Oooooh! Art history! Me too, I've always been curious about that. I wondered if you'd continued with the arts… You used to love watching the women sew back then… And your mother, how is she?"

The words drop, and Monica, who was feeling more and more comfortable with their exchange, who felt like she could open up maybe, and yes, maybe the plan had changed, closes up again. Claire is a touchy subject. Awkward even, for Monica. But she realizes she can't get around it, she can't avoid talking about it.

"I don't talk to her." She manages to say it in a voice devoid of any animosity. It's the best she can do, though her thoughts are racing. She can't know what Marie-Anne will think.

A silence takes hold, and Marie-Anne lowers her eyes, then looks at Monica's hands lying on the table. She senses her distress. "Don't feel guilty, dear. It's not your fault, you know?"

Monica's whole body suddenly relaxes. The tension vanishes, and her hands start trembling.

"Would you like a cup of tea?"

Monica nods.

Marie-Anne stands up and goes over to the stove.

She turns off the burner and takes a dishtowel hanging from a hook to pick up the teakettle. There's already a cup on the counter. Marie-Anne pours in the hot water. She dunks a bag of black tea, then comes back to the table, handing the cup to her niece. "Do you want milk, sugar?"

"Ah, yes."

"I'll bring it."

Monica is absorbed in Marie-Anne's movements. They are both determined, and at ease with each other. The time passes unhurriedly, following the rhythm of the moccasins sliding on the floor. Everything is calm outside. The sound of dogs barking is barely audible.

The old woman has something of Claire. She is smaller, however, with stooped shoulders, a silhouette like a nice old grandmother. Monica surprises herself by hoping her aunt Marie-Anne will become an Elder to her, her guide. Marie-Anne and her younger sister are thirteen years apart. Thirteen years and a world, that's the impression Monica has now, watching Marie-Anne's movements, hearing her voice, looking into her eyes.

"I think you've come to settle a lot of things, eh, my dear?" Marie-Anne remarks in her kindly voice. "But you have to take your time. You're not going to understand everything from one day to the next. One thing at a time, okay?"

Monica feels tears well up in her eyes, but as best she can she holds back the emotions that swell inside her as she hears Marie-Anne's words. She nods and grits her teeth.

"You're home now, you can smile," the old lady says, smiling. "You're already in the right place. You'll see what'll happen to you, now that you're here. Things will work out for you."

Monica suddenly thinks of Katherine outside and glances at her cellphone. She sees the message from her friend. *Take your time.*

"What's the matter?"

"Oh, nothing, it's my friend, she stayed outside. But she said she went for a drive."

"Ah, you didn't come all alone! Who's your friend?"

"Katherine. She's Anishinaabe, from Kitigan Zibi."

"Ah! Kitigan Zibi! It's been a long time since I've seen the village! When I was young, I loved to travel. Kitigan Zibi, that's where I met my first love."

"Hey!" Monica laughs. "Is that true?"

"Oh, yes! His name was Carlos. Damn, it's been a long time."

"When I go there with Katherine, I'll think of you, Auntie."

Just then, the front door opens with a loud bang. Two young children are squabbling, and a loud cry reaches the kitchen. "Mamannn!"

Marie-Anne answers just as loudly—astonishingly so, given her stature and the deep sense of peacefulness she was projecting a few seconds before. "What?"

"Can you come and get Michael, he's losing his diaper, he made me a big surprise. I wasn't expecting this now—"

An explosive laugh cuts off the rest of the sentence.

Marie-Anne scrambles up and heads down the little stairway at the front door. Monica hears her grunting as she picks up the kid, who's probably about two, before coming back up the steps with him and disappearing around a corner in the hallway. For a woman close to her sixties, she's clearly still very energetic.

Behind her, a young woman in her twenties comes into the kitchen, a little boy of about four on her hip.

As soon as she puts him down on the floor, the kid starts running toward his grandmother's bedroom.

"Kukum!"

"Hey, hi there! Ha ha ha! Excuse me, I came in yelling! I didn't think my mother had company. I'm Laurie!"

"Hi!" Monica smiles, a bit embarrassed. "My name is Monica."

"Where are you from?"

"Montreal."

"Oh, yeah? You've come quite a ways! My mother's always getting visits from all over. It's always fun!"

Laurie goes back down to get her diaper bag at the front door, then comes back up the steps and sits down on the sofa, starting to take things out of the bag one by one, sorting them as she does. The women are busy with the children, and Monica goes and sits down again at the table across from her cup of tea.

"Laurie, this is your cousin!" Marie-Anne shouts from the bedroom.

Marie-Anne reappears on the heels of the kid, all clean now, but still without a diaper, running every which way, giggling. "Look at my little scamp, running away from his grandma!"

Laurie, who is strategically positioned, catches the boy in full flight when he decides to race to his mother, spinning him around to the sound of their combined laughter.

The older child appears behind Marie-Anne and runs over to Laurie too.

"Maman, Michael hasn't got a diaper!"

It's impossible to resist the accusatory tone, and everyone joins in the laughter, including Monica.

"Ah no, we'll have to take him for his nap, tshia nituassim! He ran off without his diaper, we'll have to punish him, tshia!"

Still laughing, Laurie also takes her older child in her arms, kissing both her sons, making loud noises. "*Tan* I love them, nituassimat! They're so beautiful, my children!" she exclaims, putting her boys down on the floor. "So, Monica, the little one is Michael, and the big one is Josh."

Marie-Anne smiles broadly, standing back a bit. After another hiccup of laughter, she repeats emphatically what she was trying to say to her daughter a little earlier.

"Laurie, Monica is the daughter of your aunt Claire!"

"Huh, Auntie Claire? The one who lives in Sept-Îles, eh?"

"Yeah, that's right. She's just come back here, to Pessamit."

"My aunt?"

"No! I'm trying to tell you…it's Monica I'm talking about!"

"Ekuan, ha ha ha! I'm telling you, since I've had children, it's as if I've lost a few neurons. I must have pushed them out too hard!"

Monica is won over by Laurie's mischievous sense of humour. How old is she? Did they play together when they were kids? "Okay, I'll text my friend, see where she's gotten to."

"Do you have a place to sleep?"

"Well, we thought we'd go to Baie-Comeau."

"Nah, you can stay here, I've got an extra room downstairs. A big queen-sized bed. There's enough room for the two of you."

"Well, I don't know, I didn't want to just show up like this—"

"Stop that! It's been fifteen years since we've seen you, and you want to run off again," Marie-Anne teases, immediately easing her niece's tension.

"Okay! I'll text Katherine then. I'll tell her."

"That's good. You can put your bags downstairs, and you can stay as long as you want. This is your home too. And your friend, if she's from Kitigan Zibi, she's home here too! Innu-assi ute!"

Monica accepts the generous invitation, both amazed and surprised. Nothing has happened as she expected. And she's relieved.

In the bed, Monica's eyes are open in the dark. Beside her, Katherine is already asleep, exhausted by a day on the road, although she was buoyed by the pure pleasure of the drive. On the way to Pessamit, Monica drove a bit after they passed Quebec City, but only as far as Charlevoix. The rest of the time, her role as co-pilot gave her an opportunity to think and to consider the prospect of going back to her native village.

Katherine is such a patient and devoted friend. Monica wonders how she will ever be able to return the favour one day. She has to admit that, since they met, and not only on this trip, Katherine has been constantly leading her on the path to her own identity. Monica is aware of that now. Whatever remained of her resentment toward Katherine has finally melted away.

About a week after her return from Mexico, after several good conversations with Gabriel, who has become her informal roommate, to finally clarify her thoughts, Monica asked Katherine to meet her in a café near the university. She reminded her of everything that had happened that fateful evening, in front of Oscar, and how she had felt about what Katherine had said about Sebastian. She understood her concerns about him, she said, but it had been a mistake to rehash all that in front of Oscar in Vancouver. The whole time Monica was talking, Katherine said nothing, only nodded her head, staring at the foam at the bottom of her latte bowl. Monica, feeling relieved, told her about her experiences in Mexico and how much, during that journey, she had missed the woman she now considers her best friend. Seeing Katherine's wide eyes, astounded to find her shy friend so bold, Monica declared that, from now on, she wanted to experience all these new things with her. All these discoveries. Laughing, she made it clear that she wasn't talking about her sweet night with Maria Elena, but everything else. Everything else. And, above all, she wanted to tell her that she forgave her.

Despite that heartfelt desire for reconciliation, without intending to, she had still been carrying a bit of bitterness inside. But that was all over now.

On the other hand, she realizes there are still things that have to happen in their own time, in order to better experience them. Alone. Marie-Anne is right, she lacks answers, and she won't be able to find them all in a few days.

Monica gets caught up with imagining herself at the same age as her wise and generous aunt, except she has trouble populating the scene. She will have to reconstruct what has disappeared. But how? She doesn't know yet. Coming back here is the first step.

The day that has just gone by was wonderful. The light emanating from Marie-Anne, Laurie, and the kids touched Monica's heart. It's what she wished for herself. To one day be able to create her family... Yes, one day she will have built a community of women around her with whom she can share a filial, sororal link, the kind of family she saw today in all its splendour. Perhaps Marie-Anne and Laurie can be part of her life, and, from there, the family can be patched together again, at least a little?

I'm walking along the shore. It's raining. The night deepens, under thick grey clouds. There's not a sliver of sky to be seen, nor even fathomed. Not hoped for, nor expected. Space extends in time. Time runs out in the sand.

As for me, I'm walking. But my feet are heavy. My knees hurt. I try to take another step, with difficulty. There's no heaviness in the air, nothing but the cloud cover that weighs on my head.

I recognize the beach at Pessamit. I've spent so many summers here. I know those waves by heart, even though more than fifteen years separate us. Fifteen years, in seconds, is less than the grains of sand needed to build a castle. Gradually, the sky takes on a violet colour. The breeze tries to tug at my hair, but with uncanny slowness. And then it gets stronger, regains its force, gusts fill the space all around me. It's almost as if the wind is trying to tear off my clothes. I can't breathe anymore.

A shrill cry cuts through the air. Did I just scream? Stars break free from the clouds and fall by the thousands, straight down, toward the surface of the Saint Lawrence. Glimmers of blue.

A huge bird makes its appearance. At first I believe it is soot-coloured, but no, it's an indigo blue so dark it looks black. The crest on its head makes it look like a Great Condor, but it's even bigger than the King of the Andes. Gigantic. The wind grows stronger with each beat of its wings. The bird is giving birth to a hurricane.

It soars in figure eights from east to west above the churning waters of the Saint Lawrence, and I'm hypnotized, unable to run away. My feet sink into the beach, like I'm being sucked in by quicksand.

Suddenly, the bird changes direction, makes a last turn, offshore, before speeding straight toward me.

"Nooooo!"

This time, it's clearly me who is screaming.

I throw myself to the ground, my face in the sand, which releases my feet. I flip onto my back and notice that the clouds are once again changing colour, to a summer-afternoon pink that goes on forever.

The giant bird, which I can no longer see, screeches again. I cover my ears and open my mouth, but no sound comes out. I feel panicky but stay as still as possible. My survival instinct tells me I'll be less visible this way to the eyes of the powerful creature. My whole body curls up in fear.

And then, silence. Nothing moves. I sense that night is falling. I still have my hands over my ears, but even so I think I can hear a dull noise rising. I don't know what it is. I wait another moment. I don't want to make a move that could cost me my life if the bird is still there.

Why was I never told that Pessamit is inhabited by such a giant, dangerous creature? How can they let children play outside, without protection, when such an animal is lurking? Am I the only one who knows it's there?

After letting these thoughts wash over me for what seems like a long time, I decide to uncover my ears and lay my hands on the brown sand. Around me, nothing is moving. I look up, trembling. The sky, which barely a moment ago was filled with clouds, is clear. There are millions of stars.

I turn and see the Saint Lawrence reflecting the glimmers in the sky. It went to sleep to let the stars sparkle. The bird is gone, but instead of being reassured, I feel sad. Everything now seems dreary.

The blue light of dawn filters through the curtains of the bedroom window. Everything is peaceful, even Katherine, sound asleep on the other side of the bed. Monica blinks. She tries to hold on to the images of the dream she has just had, but she has only a feeling of anxiety and confusion.

She feels a need to go to the bathroom and throws back the sheets, although she'd love nothing more than to dive back into the dream. She gets up and walks silently along the hallway toward the bathroom. Once her bladder is relieved and her hands washed, she goes back the other way, wrapping her arms around herself to warm up a bit. It's cool in Marie-Anne's basement. The day before, after a supper livened by the antics of Laurie's children, she just trudged through the house, exhausted, to get to the bedroom. Now, curious about the memories this place might stir, she heads to the open room that occupies most of the basement. In one corner, work tables are buried under closed white boxes. Monica goes over. Among the boxes are little bags of glass beads in various colours. On a shelf on the wall, up high, sacks filled with pieces of leather await. Nearby, there's a jar with tools, which she recognizes at a glance.

Monica remembers her grandmother's skill at making moccasins, the techniques she tried to teach her a few times. Probably Marie-Anne, or perhaps Laurie, has taken up the torch. Monica also wanted to learn, more than anything. Maybe part of that longing was simply wanting to learn something of her grandmother. Yet Monica did learn something from her. It will take time before she can start studying again with someone who has carried on her grandmother's skills and who can teach her this ancient art.

She crosses the room, back to the area occupied by a television and a big sofa. Toys are scattered on the furniture and the floor. The scene conjures up a happy image for Monica. Josh and Michael have toys to play with while the women are beading beside them. The young woman tries to see if there is a clock anywhere. Her phone is still in the bedroom, and she doesn't want to wake up her friend. Not finding anything downstairs, she heads up to the kitchen, as quietly as possible.

As she tiptoes up, she looks at the walls, more closely now than she did the day before: they're full of framed photos, colour illustrations. Big eagle feathers too, and what look like sacred objects. Outside, through the sheer curtains, she can see the dawn in the distance, above the Betsiamites River.

She suddenly has an urge to go walking on the beach. Why not go and quietly watch the sunrise? She decides to make a discreet foray into the bedroom after all, and, after getting dressed, goes back upstairs and quietly leaves the house. She walks along Pisto Street toward the Saint Lawrence under a comforting blue-and-purple sky.

The street follows the curves of the little bay, which takes in the waters flowing from the Betsiamites River before letting them join the strong current of the Saint Lawrence.

The cool morning air fills Monica's lungs. Walking in this vision of the village, at five o'clock, under the first few rays of the morning sun, is like walking in a dream, almost too good to believe. Yet here she is.

After walking down Penshu Street, which intersects Pisto and goes straight to the Saint Lawrence, she comes to the sandy part of the beach. The sun is getting higher, minute by minute. Slowly but surely. There isn't really any wind, barely a few soft puffs of a breeze. Monica turns to the left, toward the orange ball that she estimates must be above the Gaspé Peninsula. Or so she guesses anyway, because during the day there's nothing visible from here of the other shore of the Saint Lawrence. It is as if there were an ocean stretching out from Pessamit. Here, the river already has the smell of the sea. It's not far from the gulf, where the water really gets salty.

Monica remembers playing on this beach with other children. Her mother is with other women sitting on towels. They are smoking cigarettes, drinking fruit juice. Late 1990s. They are young, in their early twenties. They are laughing, talking loudly. Monica is running after another child her age. She is four years old. Nearby, there is another kid, a girl—Laurie?—as well as a boy a bit older than her. They throw a little sand at each other, jump in the waves of the river. Nothing can disturb the tranquility of the children and the young mothers.

Monica savours the memory as she watches the sunrise, but the precious image evaporates when a raven appears in her field of vision, flying over the beach. She continues her walk without paying any attention to it, but it moves in the same direction as her and, when she notices it looping around again, she stops.

The raven dives smoothly and lands on the sand right in front of the young woman. It crows noisily, and Monica starts. "Shit, you scared me."

She decides to continue on her way, takes a few steps, but stops short when the raven again makes its voice heard. "What?"

The bird doesn't flinch. It starts to peck at the ground, turning its back to her.

"Scram." She starts walking again. She would like to watch the day begin without having to deal with that bird. She is mad at herself for allowing the bird to mesmerize her with its majesty. Its black plumage reminds her of Sebastian. Unworthy bird man. Except he's no longer the big, beautiful Raven for her. He's a scavenger, but without the nobility of the corvid. In spite of everything, in spite of Mexico, the echo from his husky, sad voice still haunts her sometimes, but she realizes the memory isn't painful anymore.

Katherine got her wish, Monica thinks with a smile. She warned her, she shared what she knew, she said she was worried about her friend, and Katherine managed to save her, in a way. Monica can finally see through Sebastian's game, and she's stopped looking for him at every party and waiting for his call. Has the cycle of abuse really been broken? She's not sure she'll be able to resist him, that seductive aura, if she runs into him again. And, even less, anticipate the signs that a person is the same type, potentially toxic, manipulative. Katherine won't always be there to bail her out. She'll have to learn to take care of herself.

She didn't hear the bird take off again, but it circles around her, then glides in and lands again right in front of Monica. She sees it as a confirmation that the bird approves of the path she is taking in her love life. She's on the right track. A feeling of gratitude sweeps over her.

"I believe it's time I found myself. Tshia?" she whispers

to the bird, imitating the tone that Marie-Anne adopts when she says the little Innu word: *Isn't it? Don't you agree?*

In response, the raven spreads its wings and flies off toward the forest. For an instant, Monica watches the place where it has disappeared. Out there, the trees get denser, the forest begins. She whispers a promise. "Okay. I'll go have a look there soon. Don't worry."

The sun is high in the sky now. Back at the house, Monica climbs the stairs to find her aunt Marie-Anne already sitting on the living room sofa, a steaming coffee on the table close to her, in front of a little TV set. The morning broadcast is playing at low volume, probably so she doesn't wake the children.

"Kuei, nituassim, miam a?" Marie-Anne asks sleepily.

"Kuei, Auntie."

"You went for a walk?"

"Yes, I went to the beach." Monica goes and sits down in the chair almost facing Marie-Anne, from where she has a view of the bay through the big living room window.

"How was it? It's beautiful, eh, in the morning?"

"Yes, it really is."

"I did that often, before. Now my knees hurt a little too much to go out there on foot. It's quite a walk for me."

"Marie-Anne, I wanted to ask you... Are there places where I could go, you think, to find people who could tell me what Grandma Émilie did when she was young, you know? Like, village Elders who knew her, or maybe somewhere else... I remember my mother told me she worked around Sept-Îles for a while."

Monica doesn't dare ask Marie-Anne directly. The

woman looks her niece in the eyes, and she, silent, hangs on her every word.

"Ha! Monica, when you're serious, you really have your grandmother's eyes, you know? Just now, you reminded me of my maman when she was a little older than you."

"Really? Is that true?"

"Yes, my God, I never would have imagined you'd look so much like her! Wait, I'm going to get something for you…"

Marie-Anne stands up and drags her feet to her room. Her moccasins make a sound on the floor that is utterly recognizable among all other sounds. The rhythm of her walk, familiar now, makes Monica smile.

The old woman comes back with a pair of moccasins in her hand and sets them down on the young woman's lap.

"Can you believe it? These are moccasins your grandmother made. I'm giving them to you. I've had them since she died. She still had a big bag with all kinds of moccasins, completely new. For close to twenty years we've been dipping into it, and there are still a couple left! Orders, most likely, which she didn't have time to give to the people who'd asked for them, but there's no way to know what was for who. She was sick for a long time, and you know how it is, people forget. There was also a little practice piece, something from when you were small, I think… It was wrapped in some tissue paper, with your name written on a little piece of paper. Did you get it? I came across it not long ago and sent it to you by registered mail. Laurie found your address somehow."

Monica takes in the information without showing any emotion, but on the inside, things are moving, rumbling, it's all falling into place. Of course it wasn't her mother who sent her the package. "Hey, thank you, Auntie. I'm happy to see something Grandma made."

"I'm happy too," Marie-Anne whispers emotionally. "I think I know where you can find things about your kukum. She didn't like to talk a lot about her young years, so I won't be able to help you much with that. You'll have to go to Maliotenam, to the Institut Tshakapesh. You could ask to see books or documents of hers. They'll have kept them, I think, because she worked a bit there for a while, plus she really had a knack for beading, so she showed a lot of people how to do it. Except at the time the place was called the Institut culturel et éducatif montagnais.

Monica senses that's all Marie-Anne will be able to offer her and resigns herself to a more direct approach. "Auntie…"

"Yes?"

"Did Grandma go to residential school?"

Marie-Anne's face tenses and changes completely. Her eyes fill with tears, but, remarkable woman, not a single one spills. She turns her head toward the kitchen for an instant, as if trying to choke back her emotion. Monica says nothing for a while.

"Yes, my dear…but I can't talk about it, okay?"

Marie-Anne stares at the TV screen. Monica sees how hard she's working to keep her pain from spilling out. Her face, a bit flushed, goes back to normal after a few seconds. A joke on the TV makes her chuckle, very softly. Her amused expression, while her eyes are still shining with emotion, touches Monica deeply. She certainly didn't want to cause any pain. She only needed an answer. And a destination. Now she knows.

Josh, preceded by the sound of his running feet, appears in the living room laughing and dashes over to his grandmother.

"Hello there, nituassim! Good morning!" Marie-Anne exclaims, tickling the boy.

The kid's laughter gets louder, and this time Monica joins in. "He's so funny, that kid, always happy."

"Yes! These children do me so much good, every day!" Marie-Anne says.

Laurie comes out of the bedroom too, her older child in her arms. "Good morning, girls," she says with a yawn.

"Good morning!" the two women repeat.

"He's very clingy, your Michael," Monica remarks to Laurie.

"Yes! He's always like this in the morning. He's my big baby. The other one just follows his grandmother everywhere. So cute." Laurie hands her son to Monica. The boy still smells like sleep. "Here, Michael! Go hug your auntie, I need my arms! Should I make coffee for everyone?"

"There's some already, dear," Marie-Anne replies from the sofa.

"Oh, okay. Well then, I'll make eggs for everyone."

Monica puts her arms around Michael, and, welcoming the gesture, he surrenders to the hug. Monica wants to keep that soft warmth against her, savour the moment, and especially the feeling of finally belonging to a family.

The day continued as it began: quiet, simple, joyful. That evening, Laurie cooked for everyone again. She loved having guests. When Monica expressed surprise at the gargantuan amounts of food, her hostesses explained that they always planned extra, since in the village anyone can show up for a visit without warning, and if the person is hungry, they'll sit down at the table for supper, even if the household has already eaten.

Laurie asked Monica all kinds of questions, especially about her life in Montreal. Katherine's studies and journeys were also subjects of great interest, including the recent trip to Vancouver. On Monica's initiative, the two of them even recounted the evening when they argued, Katherine doing a very convincing imitation of how she talks when she's tipsy, and both she and Monica were able to have a good laugh.

Later, to Monica's and Katherine's delight, Laurie invited the two young women to finish the evening with a campfire. The children had been put to bed, and Marie-Anne had also gone to sleep, leaving the younger women together. In the yard, a steel barrel, cut in half, was filled with branches and logs. The conversation deepened after Laurie lit the fire. Monica, who that evening was no longer afraid of talking about her childhood, surprised Katherine, enough that she listened quietly. Laurie was a clear-sighted young woman. She had barely known Claire, retaining only a very vague memory of the aunt who had left the community so soon. But since she had studied social work in Chicoutimi before taking a break to give birth to her second child in her community, some of Monica's mother's behaviour made psychological sense to her. There was an opening, and she shared her opinion, though she was careful not to suggest that the complexity of a life can be reduced to general principles. Monica, who usually felt uncomfortable hearing someone else talk about her mother, listened intently this time, trying to take in Laurie's words without any internal conflict. But something stirred inside her, like huge waves rolling on a stormy day, when she heard about the effects residential schools could have on the lives of survivors and their families.

"There were so many repercussions. It really broke people," Laurie went on. "My mother never wants to talk about it. She didn't go herself, but she once told me she knew that her mother had been to one, that's all. I was still at school, just starting, but I was seeing relationship problems that are common to many families, and often we knew that their parents had been to residential school. Anyway. My mother had told me, a bit before, how it had been hard with Claire. So I talked about it with her, so she could confirm what I felt, you know."

It was Katherine who asked Laurie to elaborate, while Monica remained silent, staring into the flames.

"And for sure Claire was affected, through her mother, right? You know, Marie-Anne, she made so much progress, she even distanced herself from her own mother for a while, because she didn't know what to do anymore, how to deal with her sometimes. But she loved her so much… Can you imagine? That's what those fucking residential schools did to our families. My mother can't talk to me about it, because she suspects what her mother went through there, I think, and it's just too much."

Laurie got a bit carried away and apologized. This always happened to her when she got on that subject, she said. Katherine suspected that the conversation was very likely to affect Monica and tried to make eye contact with her. Monica looked her straight in the eye; she was okay.

After a brief silence, Laurie continued. "I'm sorry, Monica. Maybe you weren't ready for this. I'm sorry if I upset you, I didn't mean to."

But Monica reassured her. It was hard to hear, but it

was such an important piece of a puzzle that had been unsolved for her for such a long time. "Maybe I would never have been able to see it."

Without saying any more, she starts rubbing her temples with the palms of her hands.

Maybe to permit her to resolve for herself another part of the enigma that is their family, Laurie offers Monica other bits of information.

"Well...my mother didn't tell me anything specific after, but the closest was in Maliotenam. I didn't hear that children from Pessamit were sent anywhere else, unless I'm mistaken. The building was destroyed a long time ago, but if one day you go there, you'll see."

They went quiet, listening to bubbles of sap in the fresh wood bursting in the heat of the fire and watching the sparks fly off into the night.

Then they kept chatting about this and that, lighter things, before officially declaring it was time for bed. The barrel held only glowing embers.

Monica looked up at the Milky Way just before going inside. For the first time in her life, despite the weight of the past on her shoulders and spirit, something was opening up inside her, and her heart felt freer.

For the first time, she felt like she had found her home. And it was Pessamit.

Late the next morning, Monica wakes up from a hazy vision in which, for the first time in twenty years, she thought she saw her grandmother in the dream world. Excited, she dares to wake her friend. "Katherine? Kath! Katherine! I don't think I can wait, we have to go there today, Kath! Please! Please!"

"Mmmmm...okay, but stop shaking me like that,"

Katherine grumbles, still half-asleep. "Okay we'll go."

Monica rushes out of bed, puts on pants, leaves the bedroom, and goes up the stairs.

Marie-Anne is in front of the TV.

"Marie-Anne, I'm going! I'm going to go to the Institut Tshakapesh today!"

"Okay, okay, but start with a coffee, at least, ha ha! It's already made, just grab a cup."

Monica feels at once numb, still half in her dream, and all fired up, invigorated by the conversation the day before, and also a bit excited about continuing the road trip. Buoyed by Marie-Anne's caring energy, she manages to slow down enough to pour herself a cup.

"Besides, you're only wearing one sock this morning, funny girl!" Marie-Anne chortles when she notices Monica's sock half slipping off her foot.

Monica, who hasn't realized it, laughs too. Her hair is a total mess, and the young Innu woman looks completely muddled. Marie-Anne laughs even harder, and a warm light shines from her. Making her laugh was a good distraction for Monica. It was easier not to talk to her about the real reason for their departure.

With some of the leftovers from the day before wrapped up for a picnic, and many kisses on their cheeks, Katherine and Monica set out again on Route 138.

"You know, I'm not quite sure where we're going. Is the institute in Sept-Îles?" Katherine asks an hour after their departure, the coffee finally waking up the motormouth part of her brain.

"It's in Uashat. I'll turn on the GPS, it'll be easier when we get there. For the time being, well, there's just one road. So it's straight ahead."

They both chuckle. Absent-mindedly pushing a button, Katherine opens the two front windows of the car. A change of scenery, yes, that's what they need. Since the day before, Monica has been carrying a sadness that isn't hers, though you can hear it in her breathing. The wind roars into the car, rustling the plastic of the lunch bags in the back seat.

"Wow!" Katherine shouts. "I love this so much! Wooooooooow!"

"It's the North Shore wind!" Monica laughs.

"I've never been here, I'm loving it!"

The sun is beating down, and it's hot. Monica decides to turn on the radio and look for a station with music to go with the moment. When she finally tunes in to one without too much static, she hears the first measures of "Dance Monkey" by Tones and I, which is all the rage everywhere on the planet. The two young women start singing at the top of their lungs, trying to maintain the same rhythm as the artist.

At the end of the first verse, Monica starts laughing and making *la la las* because she doesn't know the lyrics that come next. She does know the rhythm, though, and it makes her want to dance every time she hears the song. Katherine continues in unison with the artist. The day before, little Josh was singing the same tune, with everyone cheering him on. He even added a little dance, and Laurie took a video with her phone, playing the music on a mobile speaker on the table. It made for a great show, resulting in gales of laughter among the merry band. Only Marie-Anne was missing; she'd gone to town for a follow-up doctor's appointment, though she was treated to an encore when she returned.

It's only a three-and-a-half-hour drive to get to Sept-

Îles from Pessamit. The road is so beautiful under the blazing star. Summer on the North Shore, as Katherine is discovering, sparkles. She mentions this to her co-pilot.

"It's true, yes. It's true, when the weather's nice, it's really enthralling. When it's stormy too—well, only in the summer, ha ha!—it's so intense. There's almost no in-between. Even when you think it's just a neutral, cloudy, grey day, it's luminous. The sun shines through everything. And the sunsets, aah…"

"It's funny, it's as if you're describing us."

"Who? You and me?"

"Yeah, among other things, but all Indigenous women, I think."

"You think?"

"Well, in the sense that we're so invested in our emotions. Even when the people around think we're neutral, that we're feeling nothing because we don't react, well, often it's because we're shy, you know. I know women who have a gift for not showing that they're suffering, I don't know, because they want to give a nice life to their children, that kind of thing."

Monica thinks of her mother. Despite the coldness, despite the distance, yes, she did give herself, in her way. From her point of view, maybe living in Forestville, with access to education in the city, was what was best for her daughter, giving her a chance to go to university one day…except that her pain caught up with her, and it was passed down to Monica.

"Not everyone gets it quite right, I imagine, but I see your point."

They fall silent for a moment.

"Anyway, you, my beautiful Monica, I think that when you have children, you'll be a great mother."

"Huh? Why do you say that?"

"Like I was saying…when we've been through difficult stuff, we often think we won't be able to pass on the good things, the best things, to our children. But I'm sure that's not true, that it's just the opposite, for you, anyway. I was watching you with Laurie's boys… It's the most difficult things you've lived through that make you want to give the best of everything to kids. And with your own, man, it'll be crazy!"

"Yeah…I've never been sure I wanted any. But, you know, I've been watching Laurie for two days, and I tell myself, 'My God, being a mom doesn't look that hard.' Have you noticed that she hasn't mentioned the father at all? I didn't want to ask either. But that's it, it doesn't look like it's such a big challenge, especially when you love them and you're living in the moment. It seems that way anyway, I don't know."

"Yeah. So much love. I think Marie-Anne has done a good job. Laurie is lucky to have her to help with the boys anyway."

"That's for sure."

Monica wonders more about Émilie, and about Claire. Was Émilie really a mother to Claire? Did Claire get help from her to raise her daughter? She does have memories of her summers spent with her grandparents, but… what about the rest of the time? She gazes out over the Saint Lawrence, which has just appeared on their right. The opposite shore is still invisible, giving a sense of the infinite, but it seems you can see which way the currents are flowing.

She recalls Marie-Anne's eyes welling up when she asked her about residential school. It's as if she knew a lot of things, but just the idea of having to name them would have made her break into a thousand pieces.

Monica still doesn't understand the scope of the tragedy of those schools, even though Laurie provided some clues, yet when she saw Marie-Anne in that state, Monica suddenly felt like her heart was in a vise. She almost regretted her question.

When they arrive in Sept-Îles, following the directions on her phone, Monica tells Katherine to turn right. A few hundred metres farther, they arrive. The long shape of the institute for the Innu language extends before them, an unremarkable building, the only one out here, surrounded by an empty parking lot. Monica checks the time: half past noon. It must be lunchtime.

"Is this really the place where you want to go, where you think you'll learn what you want to know about your grandmother?"

Monica turns to her friend, not at all surprised by how perceptive she is. Awkwardly, she reaches across the console between their seats to put a hand on her shoulder, as if to try to transfer some of her inner discomfort.

"No. Let's go to Malio."

"Okay, but let's find a spot by the water to stop for a bite to eat. That will give us a boost, and besides, the smell of the lunch bags in the car, with the sun, you know, is starting to drive me crazy!"

"If I'm not mistaken, it's this way... There should be a wooden fence."

Katherine glances at her phone, which shows the route to the former site of the residential school. "Okay, I see."

A few seconds after the car enters the village, she slows down to the thirty kilometre per hour speed limit. The sun is still shining as the car crosses the community on one of the main streets. There are lots of people around, busy with all kinds of things on their doorsteps. Some are putting up plastic tarps to make awnings, like in a campground, with barbecues underneath. Others are hanging signs on their balconies that read *Lunch.*

"What's going on?" Katherine exclaims.

"Beats me. Everybody's getting ready for something."

As they drive by, they continue watching the inhabitants, until Katherine slows down even more and stops in front of a high fence. Several people are going in and out of an opening in the fence a little farther away. The residential school grounds must be behind it.

After parking the car, the women continue their exploration on foot. As they try to find an entrance to the site, they meet a small, happy-looking family.

"Hi!" Katherine says, speaking first to the mother. "Is there a special event this weekend?"

"Yeah, it's the start of the Innu Nikamu Festival! Isn't that why you're here?"

"Uh, yeah, among other things. When will the craft stands arrive?"

"They should be here today—well, the crafts people anyway. They'll set up tomorrow!"

"Ah, cool, okay, thank you!"

"You're welcome! Try the food in front of the houses! You'll eat well! And if you're looking for the program, it's posted all over the place."

"Hey, thanks!" Katherine replies enthusiastically, as if they hadn't just wolfed down enough to feed a whole village.

The young mother waves as her two children drag her off, followed by her boyfriend pushing the stroller with the youngest kid.

Katherine perks up. "Well, this is great!"

"Yeah! I remember now that I heard about it when I was younger. It gives another tone to our visit, but I think it's fun that we get to experience this. The festival seems kind of legendary."

"Is it? It wasn't really on my radar, I don't know why. I'm sure my parents know about it too."

"Your mother must know it!" Monica laughs.

"She definitely must have known some of the musicians. My mother was quite a party animal when she was young."

They get to an entrance to the site and go in, beaming.

Curious, the two friends walk across the grass, where a stage has been set up, ready for the show. Just as they're about to head into the enclosed space, a kind of movement starts up, and it begins to empty out around them. People are leaving the place in little groups, like they've been called elsewhere. Soon Monica and Katherine are the only ones in the middle of the site.

Monica notices a little grove of conifers along the back of the site: ancient trees—older than she is, at any rate—create a shaded, fragrant area that seems inhabited by furtive fauna. The breeze from the river blows through the pine grove, a mixture of salt and sap. In her body, everything starts vibrating. Is it nerves? Anxiety? No, she actually feels a deep calm. It's something else. A strange reaction. Suddenly, everything comes alive around her, bright colours streaming in from everywhere. They're strong, blinding lights, not just subtle sprays of colour. Monica absorbs every detail. It's as if the world were run through with veins and they were pulsing to the beat of something invisible. The effect is perceptible in her body, in her heart, which is beating very strongly. The veins hanging in the air breathe, just as she is breathing.

"Monica, are you okay?" Katherine whispers, sounding a little scared.

"I'm okay... You?"

"I...I feel something, right here, Monica."

Monica remains silent. She wonders if she should ask Katherine the question, knowing that her friend is fearful of any supernatural manifestations outside of the reassuring setting of ceremonies. But why can't she learn not to be afraid of energies beyond what she knows? "Katherine?"

"Huh?"

"Do you see it too?"

"Well...um..."

Katherine opens her eyes wide, alarmed, her fear going up a notch. She did notice that everyone left just when they got to the middle of the site. *What a coincidence!* When Monica slowed down, then stopped completely, she thought she felt a presence, yes. But without a guide, without references, she can't know if it's benevolent or the opposite. Her hands start to shake. She becomes aware that she is not alone, that there is, in fact, someone to open up the path for her here.

"Tell me what you see, Monica. Be honest."

"Won't you be afraid?"

"Yes, but no! I trust you." Katherine lets a silence settle, calms her breathing until it's inaudible.

Monica tries to maintain contact with her vision. She's afraid the tiniest movement will make her lose her contact.

"I think you didn't only come back for you."

Katherine's words touch Monica's heart, as if she had

been waiting for them since the beginning. She feels something that she recognizes, that unravels; a warmth rises in her body from the ground, in her feet, rolling around in her belly, climbing to the roots of her hair.

Time and space have opened up for both of them. Monica closes her eyes. Katherine, still trembling, stands bravely beside her friend. She decides to take another step toward her and puts her hand on her shoulder. Looking all around her, she thinks she sees shadows floating by. The shapes are far from opaque, but it's as if they're perceptible somehow throughout the festival site.

"It's as if everything was connected, Katherine. It's in our bodies. Our nerves run throughout our bodies. And in the universe, even in what we don't see—especially in what we don't see—everything is connected. If we breathe, the universe breathes too."

"I know what you mean."

"I've never felt that before."

Katherine smiles to herself, standing behind Monica. Seeing herself in this position with her best friend, she thinks they must have come together so she can become her partner, her guide, but also the one who will help her find her identity and her own power.

Monica suddenly feels a very familiar presence. "Katherine! Do you feel that? Like a warm hand over your heart."

"What? No, Monica. That's just for you, I think. I've been seeing the shadows of children since we got here, though. The past is heavy here, it's all around me."

"Yes, but it's more specific than that." Monica, her eyes still closed, can't hold back the tears. She remembers so clearly being blanketed in her kukum's warmth as soon as she saw her, even from very far, on Ashini Street. She had forgotten that feeling, the feeling of loving a person so much that there's a sense of fullness in that love. She's a little girl once again, in Émilie's arms.

"Kukum…?"

Her lips quiver as sobs rack her body. Monica feels a great joy come over her, and then, suddenly, an immense pain runs through her, pressing down on her shoulders. She drops to her knees and starts to sob even harder.

Katherine immediately bends over her, glances around, trying to see, to feel. An Innu man emerges from behind the stage in the distance. He walks a little in their direction, but his eyes meet Katherine's, and she signals to him not to come closer. Understanding that he should leave them alone, he walks away.

Katherine tries to get Monica to sit down, and notices her watch: it's five-thirty. All the employees probably left at the same time to go home for supper. She strokes her friend's back, upset by Monica's convulsing body. Katherine, who often senses what others feel, knows that Monica has just had a strong experience. What Monica is lamenting at this very moment is the weight of the residential schools.

If Monica's grandmother did, in fact, experience atrocities like those that have been talked about for many years, including the revelations that tore at her heart during the Truth and Reconciliation Commission hearings, which she followed closely, Katherine can imagine the weight of trauma her friend must carry.

Katherine thinks about her parents, their long journey of healing. That's why she knows the ceremonies, because she grew up in a world where people from all over the continent came to visit her father and her mother to ask for help through the ancient rites of her people. They were sent to residential school too, each during a different time of their lives.

When her father was a child, his parents would go deep into the woods every year to get away from the RCMP officers and social services agents. But later, as a teenager, he was forced to go with the government representatives, who caught him just before his family ran away in the summer. He wasn't one of those who suffered most at the hands of the priests, he had reassured Katherine. And he was one of several young men who helped protect the little ones, scheming to ensure not a single one disappeared at night.

Katherine's mother wasn't spared, however, and endured all kinds of abuses. Saw all kinds of things. It took years before she was able to stop seeing life in terms of what she had witnessed, which taught her about the worst in human beings. Anishinaabe ancestral spirituality gave her great solace. She recounted to her daughter that day when she knew, when she felt in her heart, that the best path to healing was to find what they had tried so hard to erase: spirituality and the traditional rites. Despite the views of others in the village and in other Nations, she fought to learn and, when the time came, to provide that healing for the spirits of the people from her Nation.

And that was what happened. The two met at a traditional gathering and set out together on a bumpy road of joys and sorrows. They had four children: Katherine is their only daughter, with three older brothers. She never had a sister; maybe that's why she's always been very maternal toward her friends. She often feels an urgent need to protect, to guide, to give advice, not that any of that stopped her, in her own journey, from making all the mistakes of youth, all kinds of dumb things. She often tells herself that she perhaps gets that protective instinct from her parents. A bit of the legacy of the residential schools that they passed down to her without realizing it. All of it comes to her at that instant, in a flash.

And she's here, consoling her friend. Now Monica is crying softly. Katherine can sense from Monica's body that letting out the tears did her good. She knows that Monica is already a lot more relaxed.

Things are picking up again at the entrances. Employees are gradually coming back from their evening meals, returning to set up the festival site.

"Come," she whispers to Monica.

She stands, and Monica follows. They walk slowly to the car. The sun has sunk a little lower in the Maliotenam sky, and the colours are changing from blue to purple and orange. Today was a hot day, and tomorrow will be too.

The next day was the opening of the festival, and the community was in high spirits. Katherine and Monica decided to stay, and woke to the sound of the celebrations beginning. They hadn't found a place to sleep at first and called Justin, who had made calls here and there to his family in the region to ask how the preparations for the festival were going and see who still had a bed free. Finally, Katherine and Monica ended up at the home of one of Justin's relatives, a cousin, who told them she would be happy to host them for the whole weekend.

After notifying a delighted Marie-Anne of the change in plans and telling her about the festival—to which Marie-Anne exclaimed, *Ah, yes, it's true, the festival! Have a good time!*—they got caught up in the spirit of things. During two magical days, Monica discovered many artists, both Innu and from other Indigenous cultures. There was non-stop music and constant smiles, laughter, and dancing. There were endless bands to be heard, and guitars, the voices...almost all of it in Innu-aimun. They heard other Indigenous languages of Québec and beyond, too, from artists involved in their communities or their nations, who had come here in a spirit of communion.

The experience they had on the site stayed with Monica, and she thought back a lot to her grandmother as she stood in the crowd in front of the stage pulsating with life. On the Saturday evening, fireworks had lit up the sky, and exclamations of surprise and joy rang out all around her, but also deep in her belly.

Here in Maliotenam, by reclaiming their culture and their songs, the Innu truly accomplished something year after year. Monica was elated and promised herself she would return every year to celebrate not only her Innu culture but also the healing power of that heritage.

I've lived in the city for six years already. Six years during which I've buried myself under concrete to get away from that call inside my chest. That's how it goes.

How will complete healing ever be possible? I've asked everyone about it, but not in so many words. I know we will seek the answer everywhere. We will give it all kinds of names. We will stir up so much. We will think we were ready.

If we don't find an answer, we will imagine it in the dark eyes of anyone. We will fall into their souls. There will be no ground, only an infinite sea. An ocean. No islands. No sky. Nothing but the storm. And we will be stuck there.

Healing sometimes means leaving. Going away. Running away? Running away. To never return.

I've looked for you for such a long time. Light.

You were waiting for me there. It's as if there were moments of brightness that only lasted awhile. How many more?

I forgot, for so many years. The return carried with it the fear of seeing only darkness. That you were gone, that you had left my people. That it was all only a dream, like the real ones that invade my nights.

I turn the car onto Ashini Street when the star is at its highest point in the sky. Katherine and I left Maliotenam in the morning so we would have the whole afternoon ahead of us, once we dropped off our luggage at Marie-Anne's house. Just one more week until we return to Montreal, and we want to make the most of the time we have.

In Pessamit, we go past the convenience store at the entrance to the village and turn right to take Kesseu, then go to Pisto Street on the left, farther on. We drive past my grandmother's house, and I see lights on inside. I don't know why, but I think of candles.

"Katherine?"

"Yeah?"

"Would it bother you to unload everything on your own, then come join me on the beach in a little while? I'm going to go to my grandmother's house, I think. I can get out here, no need to take me to the door."

"Um, yeah, if you like. Why, who's living there now?"

"I'm not sure. It seems like there's somebody there. I think my mother's here for the festival."

"You think?"

"Yeah."

"How do you know?"

"She did that when I was little. We'd come and stay at her mother's house, every year, for the week of August 15."

"I get it."

Katherine doesn't add anything, doesn't risk another question. I see it in her eyes. I'm getting to know her. Yes, Katherine, I think I'm going to see my mother.

I undo my seat belt and get out. I lean over to see my friend better. She nods, looking straight into my eyes, then drives off.

In front of the front door, I take a little book from my handbag. I've never shown it to anyone, not even Katherine.

Suddenly, I'm overcome with nervousness. My heart is pounding. It feels like there is no more blood in my body, except in my chest. I try to keep calm, to control my heartbeat, but it keeps accelerating. It's been fifteen years since I've been back to this house. It might as well have been centuries. I've always had the feeling that it was forbidden after we left the village. The last moments spent under the same roof as my grandmother and my mother are fuzzy, as if, because of the pain, my memories had diminished, worn away by time, the way an old photo loses its shine. My mother's name is Claire, but at the age of seventeen, in my own mind, I nicknamed her Fog instead. Impossible to see through. She was a cliff of tears, my mother, so hard on herself and others, but at the same time so hard to pin down. I could never take her in my arms.

I've been standing in front of the door for too long, I realize. Neighbours have likely noticed me already. *What's she doing here? Who is she? We don't know her.* No doubt they're behind their curtains, looking out the windows at me. Watching my every move.

I put my hand on the doorknob and turn it, finally opening the door. As soon as I step inside, I hear a voice and my whole body reacts. I almost jump. Almost dash out the same door that let me in. There's nothing in my way. It should have kept me from entering the dark part of my psyche.

"Uene?"

My eyes sweep around the room. The living room. I recognize objects that belonged to my kukum. Decorations still hanging on the walls. The old glass ashtray stand is still there, even though no one has smoked here in a long time. It's been in the same spot for twenty years.

"Who's there?"

Her voice echoes faintly again in the hall.

I go from the living room to the kitchen, where a door leads out to the backyard. An emergency exit, just in case.

I see Claire. As soon as she notices me, she stops short.

"Nituassim…nituassim. My child." When she calls me that, a huge black hole opens in my belly, growing into my throat, until it erases my uterus.

My hands are shaking. I tuck them behind me, gripping the book to keep them still. The book I brought her. I will show her nothing.

Claire is silent. I don't know what to say. I look deep into her eyes. An ocean of anger roils there. A new storm is brewing deep in my guts, an ocean I thought was calm now. Of course not. A hurricane could still come crashing down on Pessamit.

"I didn't come to chat…"

"So why did you come then?" Claire says, sharp, mercurial, as usual.

She turns away from me and goes behind the counter. Stops. As if she wanted to protect herself from something. She frowns. I recognize my mother's reactions all too well, all her nuances, her complexity. Claire is unsettled, except that her great sense of pride still makes her hide her feelings.

I stay standing proudly. I don't give in.

I had been missing something, an element that was so important for my understanding of life, my own existence. Why Claire is the way she is, why so much pride, so much suffering, so much nastiness.

Envy.

Claire always tried to take back what she had just given.

Youth, beauty, the joy of living.

Claire gave me everything. But from one day to the next, things were turned upside down when she fought with her own mother, Émilie. Then everything had changed. Our lives became a tug of war between mother and daughter.

All that, in my belly. And in Claire's belly? How can I know, since she's kept all the doors of her spirit locked up tight for such a long time, shutting herself off in a dark tower where no one can come and find her?

There is a voice inside me.

Maman, what happened to you?

That question cuts through me. Now the tears start welling up.

To understand my mother, I have to understand my grandmother. I remember the enormity of the pain in Marie-Anne's eyes. Immeasurable. So much like the pain

I felt around me at the site of the residential school, the children's pain, Émilie's.

Little Émilie, so fragile, defenceless. She had nothing, with no one.

Claire never knew how to be a mother because Émilie didn't know how to be one either.

And it wasn't her fault.

The residential schools broke all three of us, one generation after the other.

In my body, everything adjusts. My spine cracks audibly. My rib cage, my femurs, my tibias. Everything.

"Maman…"

My voice is trembling, but I don't want a voice that trembles. I draw unimaginable strength from I don't know where to keep myself from giving in to the urge to weep.

Claire doesn't turn around. She's frozen, a still life painting.

I am seized by doubt. Is she real?

I refuse. The storm in my belly is too real for me to be dreaming it.

"Maman…listen to me!"

Claire turns to me with teary eyes, eyes filled with desperation and pain, infinite sadness. A lost, abandoned child. She has the eyes of someone who can't find her way home.

My heart falters.

"Maman, I want to tell you…"

"Nituassim é…"

My mother's voice. I'm going to give in.

"What…?" I'm crying. I can't help it.

"Nituassim…"

"What!"

Claire tilts her head, all alone in her corner of the kitchen, her back to me. "Forgive me, okay...?"

She covers her face with her hands. Slowly, her vertebrae proliferate. Her spine bends. Her hair, blacker than night, changes, grows long and turns whiter than snow. Her skin is suddenly greyish. She grows tall, her back touches the ceiling, which soon is much too low for her.

"Yes, Maman, I forgive you."

Claire starts sobbing. The whole kitchen trembles. Artifacts from another era slide off the shelves and walls. Everything shatters. Everything smashes on the floor. I panic, I try to catch a few souvenirs. Pieces of us.

The earth trembles. I put on the table the book I brought to give Claire.

My poems.

I spin back to the door, open it, and I leave. I walk, then start running through the streets. I'm crying uncontrollably.

It takes me a few minutes to get to the end of Laletaut Street, where there is a crucifix, facing east. Seeing the figure of Jesus, I start running even faster. Like the wind, I sprint down the slope leading to the beach. I leap over a little stream and I keep going.

"Claire!" I shout her name. Where do spirits go who have suffered so much? I'm sure I could call back her broken spirit by shouting into the air. I'm sure residential school survivors, and their children, have souls broken into pieces, countless fragments floating in the air everywhere in the country, across the continent. We could all start running, we, their children, we, their grandchildren, grab those little nets for catching butterflies, and go off in search of the parts of their souls. Bring them home.

And after, we will use those little nets to fish for salmon. All of us together.

That cry reminds me of my very first one, revives the memory of my own birth: "Kukum!"

I fall to the ground.

"It hurts!"

My tears keep flowing. The sun is shining. There's no wind. Everything is calm.

But I am not alone, writhing under the hot sun.

I hear a scream. It's not mine, but it is coming from underneath me. A baby. Gleaming. Covered in blood.

It's still connected to me by the umbilical cord. I take my child in my arms. I wipe away my tears. I quake with astonishment. I've given birth. I have to take care of my baby. I remember that we don't name children before knowing if they identify as boys or girls, or neither. That's the way it was before the white people came.

I notice their gaze. Their eyes. I would know them anywhere. "Kukum?"

Monica wakes up with a start in the bed, sweating, and the movement wakes Katherine, who sits up too. Lost between realities, Monica starts sobbing.

Katherine is groggy, but her heart breaks for her weeping friend, and she takes her in her arms to stroke her, to rock her against her heart. There is darkness all around her. "Hush, hush, hush, my friend, it's okay, my dear friend… Hush…"

She rocks Monica slowly, pressing her against her body for several minutes, until she finally falls asleep again. When she senses that Monica is sound asleep, exhausted by crying, Katherine goes back to sleep too.

Before dawn, Monica leaves the house with one thing in mind: to go watch the sunrise over the Saint Lawrence. She takes the path to the west, past the crucifix at the end of Laletaut, and walks on to the beach.

Half an hour later, Monica is still walking along the shore. She must be more than five kilometres east of Pessamit.

In the distance, she notices a silhouette against the shadows, on the edge of the woods, working next to a big canoe upside down on stilts. As she approaches, she starts making out an old Innu man, heavy-set, not very tall. She decides to go over to him.

"Kuei," she greets him when she is still a few metres away.

The old man is busy working the wood on top of a stump. He turns to her and, under the rays of the rising sun, squints to better see the face of the young woman who has spoken to him.

"Kuei, miam a?" he says in a colourless voice.

"Yes, I'm okay. May I ask what you're doing?"

"I'm fixing my canoe."

Monica watches as he continues working. Her presence doesn't seem to bother the man, whose face is creased with deep wrinkles. "Do you live here, sir?"

"Yes, I'm always here."

"You mean you live in the woods there, all alone?"

"I've been doing this my whole life." He stops his work to look again at Monica's face. He studies her for a long time, still squinting. "Can you stop being so formal?" he says, catching her off guard.

"Um, yeah, okay."

"I must seem pretty old, eh?"

"Well…yeah," Monica stammers. "How old are you

178

actually?"

"Seventy-three."

Monica is dumbstruck.

The Innu man responds to her silence with a big belly laugh. "Ussen, come now! I don't feel old, I *am* old."

The Innu man keeps laughing alone, laughing even harder at this last statement, delighted with his own joke.

Monica, initially ashamed, understands that he's teasing her and starts to laugh with him too. "Wow, he must be…" she whispers to herself.

"I love to tell that joke, I always get people with it. You can sit down if you like. What's your name?"

"Monica."

"Okay, I'm George."

"Hi, George."

"Hi… Ish… Kuei! Come now, you have to say kuei. Where are you from?"

Monica is unsettled again by George's directness. "Uh, Montreal."

"Montreal? I thought you were from here."

"Well, my family is."

"Oh yeah? Who's your mother?"

"Claire Hervieux."

"Claire Hervieux?" The man is silent for a moment, then takes out a cigarette from a pack on the stump beside him. As soon as he has lit it, he turns again to Monica to study her face. "And your grandparents were…"

"Well, there was Émilie Hervieux, my grandmother. And, Philippe Bacon, my grandfather…"

"Émilie Hervieux, eh… Okay…I can see it. You look a heck of a lot… It's like looking at her when she was your age."

Monica finds it a little hard to believe she's with a

man who knew her grandmother when she was a young woman. Something led her here, to answers. George inspires confidence, and she pushes on, toward the next stage she needs to go through. Her promise to the raven, made on another sunrise. "I want to go into the woods. Can you help me?"

George looks at her again, examining her from head to toe. "Yes, we'll go, but we have to wait until the end of September, or even October, if you want to be sure of your shot."

Monica's first impulse is to ask why it's not possible to go there now, today. But she catches herself, the memory of Émilie in her heart. It will take time. "I can wait."

The old man takes a moment to think in silence. Then he agrees. "Okay. I'll get my people together, and we'll leave at the beginning of October, okay? Come back to see me then. I'll be ready."

Monica can barely contain her excitement, take in what has just been agreed to, what's going to happen, what remains to be done. "So, you…uh, you knew Émilie?"

The man looks up at her, his dark eyes shining in the light of day. His cigarette hangs from his lips like an accessory. Monica waits for his answer, her eyes wide open.

"I'm really happy to meet you, little one. I knew Émilie when I was young, you can guess how long ago that was," he begins. "You know, she was so beautiful… Even today, I often think of her, of our years together. I was always in love with her, even when I was little, I think."

Seeing Monica's stunned expression, the old man starts laughing heartily.

"That's love, eh. Especially, I think, love over time. Today, it's as if people don't love like before. People don't love for so long. With us, back then, it was like, when you fell in love, it was for life. Even if life separates you, you're still in love. And after, you make your life without ever forgetting."

Monica sits on a log close to the man and his canoe. He continues carving what looks like a tool from a piece of wood with his little knife, without ever taking his cigarette out of his mouth. He smokes like that, his hands busy working the wood.

A light wind visits Monica and her new acquaintance, while the sun rises higher and higher. Everything is calm, even the waves, as if the whole world wants to wrap this exchange in tranquility, Monica thinks to herself. More and more, she has the feeling that, in this village and all around, things are not only strange, but magical. She could swear that animals talk; the sounds they sometimes produce for human beings make it seem like they communicate with ease. Only Monica, who didn't grow up here, didn't live here long enough, does not know the language of the people of Pessamit. But she will learn. She is already learning.

A branch cracks behind her, and Monica whirls around. Nothing. She doesn't see anything. But like the other time with Katherine, she has the distinct feeling someone is coming toward them.

She recognizes a familiar smell: raspberries. Berries gathered in the woods. Memories from her childhood... She sees herself getting out of her grandmother's pickup, a big pickup truck, close to their cabin in the woods. They lift the little empty pails and head out on the dirt road to find raspberries.

"George? How long were you in love with my grandmother?"

The old man looks up at her, gazing into her eyes. He smiles with a charm that moves Monica deeply. "Just before she died, I'd redeclared my love for her!" he chuckles. "I felt like telling her again how much I had loved her my whole life. I'd found out not long before that she was sick, you know. I wanted her to know that, even though we couldn't be together, well, that she was loved. And that she was going to be loved even when she was gone."

These words strike a chord with Monica. The old man tries to hide his eyes, his emotions, under the visor of his green cap.

"I'll tell you as much as you want. Well, as much as I know. There must be stories you haven't heard."

"Yeah, really. It's as if...as if something is asking me to go looking for her. I don't know how to explain it."

"There's no need to explain everything, ishkuess. When we go into the woods, you'll see. You'll understand that we don't need to explain things."

The words make Monica shiver. It's as if she already understands, but at the same time she knows that only in the forest will she really be able to grasp the full meaning of his words.

Behind them, above the water, a buzzard goes by. A few wing flaps, then it pirouettes and comes to a standstill in the sky. The world is suspended.

It's finally October.

Monica has been counting the days, even though no precise date had been set.

She had hung around George's cabin, hoping to worm a little more information out of him, and when she asked him if the departure date was at all clear to him, all he answered was, *When you feel it's time, you'll come back, and I'll be waiting for you.*

She saw him again, on the beach, a little later in September, when she was still meditating on those words, which would follow her for the rest of her life. That day, he had shown her on a map the Manicouagan Reservoir and the waypoints that would mark their journey. When she dared express a bit of concern about the distance they had to cover, he assured her, a twinkle in his eye, that the destination was worth the effort. Monica didn't push it. Instead, she decided to strengthen her arms and her back for the journey. And to do some work on Marie-Anne's house, which needed a few odd jobs, guided by Laurie, who knew what to do.

When the date of the planned return to Montreal came, Katherine went on alone, promising Monica she would help Gabriel take care of the cat and the plants; everything would be fine. Monica felt that her friend was holding back: recommendations, warnings—tears too, perhaps. But Katherine had understood that Monica had to do this next part of the trip without her. She gave her a big hug and left. Since Katherine's departure, they sometimes exchanged messages on Facebook, but except to give her friend news or to write to Oscar, Monica stayed away from the screen, too busy preparing physically for what lay ahead.

And now autumn has come, and Monica is sitting in that pickup truck with people she barely knows, having only seen them sometimes in the village when it was her turn to go shopping with Marie-Anne. Monica remembers her aunt telling her they were the ones working hard for Innu culture. In the community, they were often on the front lines, getting involved on cultural days or for collective projects. Three big vehicles filled with all the material necessary drive one behind the other on Route 138. Each truck carries a big canoe, two red and one dark green. Monica thinks back to her extended stay in Pessamit. She's so glad she and Katherine spent the last hot days of summer on the river, Monica familiarizing herself with navigation and refining her paddling techniques with Laurie, who really seemed to appreciate those moments between cousins, while Marie-Anne took care of the boys. On more than one occasion, her aunt told her that as soon as the kids were big enough, she wanted to take them out on the land, to experience the same journey Monica was about to undertake.

A long, picturesque road stretches out before her now. Monica, who has rediscovered it during short trips up over the last few months, anticipates the curves.

Sitting in the front seat of the third vehicle, on the passenger side, she watches the houses going by, the view opening up from time to time on the Saint Lawrence, the load in the pickup in front of them. It's eight o'clock, and the people on board are just as silent as she can be in the morning. There are occasionally murmurs, technical questions, little bursts of laughter. The coffee still hasn't kicked in. Everyone got up very early to get ready.

Monica stares at the road, which seems to swallow up the pickup in front. She recalls scraps of her life, as if they were mixed with the material of the road, and meditates this way until Baie-Comeau, where they pick up Route 389, which will take them north, toward the Manicouagan Reservoir.

When they begin that segment of the trip, Monica suddenly sees again all the events of the last months that brought her here. Everything that has shaken up her life.

She sees her grandmother, the moccasins, the big, gentle hands sewing and embroidering flowers or Innu patterns on the leather.

She sees her mother, in her loneliness, certainly in her distress at not having a mother who could fulfill her own needs as a child, as a teenage girl. Who, when she herself became a mother, doubted herself still. She sees again her own adolescence, her endless conflicts with Claire, her anger and pain, amplified by the anger and pain of the two women who came before her, who had each hoped, in offering a daughter to the world, to be able to rebuild what was broken in them.

And here she is, Monica, on the road toward their ancestral Innu lands.

She's the one who is starting to rebuild.

Every bump in the road is a reminder of the number of times she was told, *Your mother loves you*. And each time she feels the fire in her belly.

I have been trying to heal for so long, except I didn't know the path of pain, and I know I have to take it to get to the other side, to leave behind what lives on in me, the anger.

But its face and texture have changed.

This is no longer the same anger that has been driving me for almost my whole conscious life, the anger born of not being loved as I wanted to be, as I needed to be.

Now I am angry because I know that places have been created to erase the existence of my people, of all First Peoples. Those who conceived that monstrous plan weren't successful, but, in some cases, they were able to crush entire lives and damage many more. How many were promised love and tenderness, and received none?

Even though connections are broken in my family, I found my grandmother in space-time. Somewhere in the cosmos, my link with her has crossed the years, our stories, our wounds, our scars. It has spanned the impossible.

Like that piece of leather the two of us sewed with strands of colour. It crossed the twenty years that separate me from her, to give me a direction again. Émilie was in my life, just enough for a spark.

What remains for me, deep in my heart, is the question I've been asking myself ever since my search in Malio and Sept-Îles: If not for residential school, would she still be alive? What killed her in the end was lung cancer. As if she had spent her whole life short of breath. Trying to breathe. Trying to keep her head above water...

I think it will take me another century or two before I finish asking questions. Before everything is clear. Except I believe that, today, I'm on the right track. I don't remember ever feeling that before. Now I just have to discover the most important thing.

On the land.

Nutshimit.

Innushkuess u nin. Yes, I remember those words.

It's coming back to me.

After driving for six hours, the three vehicles finally arrive on the shore of a calm little river, at the spot where they will put the canoes into the water and load them with all the material necessary for the expedition.

As soon as the trucks are parked, everyone gets out to begin the work. There are only two women in the group, out of a total of six. In addition to Monica, the team is made up of George, their guide, plus his son, two of his nephews, and the wife of one of them.

Bag after bag of dried food, tools, and clothes—everything is unloaded, checked, then loaded into the canoes and secured with long yellow ropes, with knots to which only the members of George's family hold the secret.

Monica tries to pitch in, working as best she can, but is astounded by the speed with which the canoes are filled and the efficiency with which all the baggage is stowed, while all she does is carry supplies over to the canoes. Soon there's no space in the boats, except spots for the people in the group, two per canoe. They have already explained to Monica that the women will sit in the bow of their respective canoes, in accordance with tradition. Monica will paddle with George's son Jean-Louis, while George will be with Camil, the older of his nephews, and the younger, Rich, will be in the third canoe with his wife, Annie.

The men get in first to hold the stern steady. Sitting in the back of his canoe, George signals to Camil to get in, then they both paddle their canoe closer to the one in which Monica is still looking for a stable position. George's dark eyes look deep into hers, and the old Innu gets her to make a few movements in the air to ensure that she knows the different ways to use the paddle to properly manoeuvre her canoe, both to propel it and in case of emergency.

Monica congratulates herself on not having waited until now to train. Everyone is anxious to get going and, just a few minutes later, the boats are moving through the water.

The river isn't very wide, the current is not too fast, and Monica finds manoeuvring easy enough and quickly gains confidence. Her canoe mate, who is a little older than she is but far more experienced, paddles with a slowness that is not only reassuring but reminds her that here there is nothing to mark the passage of time except for their movements and those of nature around them.

The sun is still high. We have time to cover a good distance before sunset. We have to take the time to travel.

The weather. The weather is good, neither cold nor hot.

The canoes slide effortlessly through the water. Monica is struck by the tranquility of the surroundings. Everything is silence, except that the silence is made up of the subtle sounds of animals hidden from their eyes, insects, movements on either side of the waterway, leaves moving on the branches of the trees.

I go against the current of the rivers. My heart follows the rhythm of the rapids, their everlasting flow. Pulling upstream is waking all the pain in my body. Paddling, plowing through the waters. I am an Innushkueu sitting in the front of her first canoe. The Innuat follow me with a spirit akin to the grace of migrating salmon, in slow motion. They are behind me, my guides in the afternoon light.

The hours go by, and you barely notice. Out here, you really forget that there are hours, clocks, calendars.

"That raven has been following us for a while now," Jean-Louis remarks softly.

Monica turns and spots the raven a short distance behind them. The bird flies from tree to tree, apparently matching the speed of the little group.

"I saw it when we left, but I didn't realize it was following us."

It's Jean-Louis who has just made this observation. Monica is speechless. Emotions catch in her throat, though she tries to suppress them. She is the one the bird has been following, since Pessamit!

George's canoe passes hers, and Monica momentarily meets the old man's inquiring eyes. Not wanting to share her disquiet, she tries to turn his attention to something else. "Oh, look there! Is that a loon?"

Monica points to the right. The waterway widens into a lake and, a ways away, they can make out a loon, its plumage ranging from grey to green to a rusty orange. It's amazing even to those who are accustomed to seeing them.

"I think we can stop here for supper," Jean-Louis says, pointing to the little beach beyond the loon.

The sun is setting. The temperature has dropped, and a chilly wind comes up. If they stay on the water, they'll start shivering. The moment is well chosen.

"Good idea, it'll do me good to stretch my legs!" Rich agrees, immediately steering the canoe he's sharing with

Annie in that direction. "I don't want to eat peanuts for the whole trip!"

Laughter rings out in the cool air of the boreal forest.

They steer to the sandy shore, slowly climb out of their canoes, and pull them up the beach.

The brothers, Camil and Rich, get started assembling a little circle of stones for the fire. Everyone is busy with something. George carries his knives to the place where the meal will be prepared, while Monica unfolds a camping chair so the old man will be able to sit comfortably, and Jean-Louis and Annie set up the tents and gather kindling. Monica is asked to get out the food. The meat, taken from the freezer a few hours earlier, should have had enough time to thaw. Monica is silent, watching every movement of the others, learning.

This first supper is eaten with good humour and wild laughter, led mostly by Jean-Louis and Rich, who are particularly good at telling silly jokes.

"I can't stand it," Monica says, hiccupping. "I'm not sure anyone can survive here laughing like this!"

She has a feeling of contentment, simply from being with them all. One laugh at a time, she is making up for so many years of deprivation. She hadn't known that what was absent was so simple, that it had been part of the daily lives of Innuat since forever. Her people, since forever.

When the supper things are cleaned up and everyone can finally take the time to rest, Monica goes down to the river's edge to sit down, to look at the silhouette formed by the line of spruce trees as the sun vanishes behind them.

The relative solitude allows her to take in every detail. Several rivers flow into the lake where they've stopped, which is huge. On the far side, cliffs and sandy slopes soar above the expanse of water. Birds, unidentifiable from so far away, fly over the tips of the fir trees. On the horizon to the southeast, Monica notices a cluster of grey clouds, high in the sky and thick, extending as far as the eye can see. The humidity has been rising, especially during the last hour.

Maybe it will rain later in the evening, Monica thinks. Or else tomorrow. She imagines the rest of their trip, canoeing in the rain. Already, this afternoon, it wasn't easy getting used to paddling so much. Fortunately, George chose calm rivers to allow her to gain some experience. Monica closes her eyes. She sees again all the landscapes that have surrounded them throughout the day. She goes back over each conversation, and each silence too.

Opening her eyes again, she turns her gaze to the water. The calm. Close to her feet, tiny waves roll pebbles over her toes. She counts the kilometres that separate her from home. Or, rather, from Tio'tia:ke/Montreal. From her cat, from Katherine, from Gabriel and the others. There, everything still needs to be built. Here, everything is being built around her.

Monica stands on the shore. The sky is a strange colour. Between dark grey, blue, and violet. Flashes of lightning cut through the clouds. The brightness of the lightning burns Monica's fascinated eyes. Each time, she is briefly blinded, and her retina retains an ephemeral trace of the fire in the sky.

A rumble reverberates across the whole territory. The trees bend, and the sound travels through space, making every living thing tremble. The waters are stirred up, forming giant rings, which Monica doesn't know how to react to. Should she stay or run?

A celestial cry rings out. The wind comes in great gusts, so powerful that Monica has trouble standing up straight. She bends over a bit, reaching toward the ground in case she falls if the earth shakes again, or ready to throw herself down if some catastrophe should occur.

The colours of the clouds suggest every scenario is possible. However, even though it seems as if the face of the world is about to be torn away, Monica feels a tranquility she's never known before.

A familiar feeling—yes, she is reassured by a sense of déjà vu.

With a great crash of thunder, the sky opens up and a giant bird appears, beating its huge wings, which lift it high above in the blink of an eye, so high that soon it's the size of a fledgling.

Monica watches the flight of the gigantic animal. It banks to one side, lets itself fall, and starts to plunge toward the expanse of water.

She wonders briefly if she should lead the others to shelter. Of course not: she has to stay, to bear witness.

The bird hits the surface at an insane speed, and its weight creates a wave that envelops Monica in its loving arms.

The flames crackle in the darkness, lighting up the faces of those who are still awake, warming themselves around the fire. Rich, Annie, and Camil are already bedded down. Only Monica, George, and Jean-Louis are still sitting by the campfire. George talks about the weather they've had since they left Pessamit and shares his thoughts about what this journey means for him. He tells them what he saw around here when he was very young and what no longer exists. For twenty years, he says, he never came back inland. But for the past thirty years now, he has arranged to return each year, accompanied by whoever wants to go that fall.

"Without this, we are in danger of losing our knowledge. If we lose our knowledge, we lose a part of our Innu identity."

Jean-Louis nods as George is speaking. His silence is the silence of a man who is continuing to learn, to receive, and, above all, to let his Elder speak to ensure the transmission of knowledge and visions. There has been an atmosphere of respect since George began his monologue on the subject of knowledge. Like Jean-Louis, Monica is all ears, captivated both by what their Elder is recounting and by his unique way of speaking. Despite his age, despite his gentleness, George gives off an impressive aura of power.

"And you, Monica…did you notice a raven following us ever since we arrived in the territory?" George's voice floats above the fire.

Monica, who for a few moments let herself get caught up in the flow of thoughts going through her mind, starts when she hears George mention the bird. Taken aback, confused, incapable of putting into words what she believes she knows of this presence hanging over her, she only nods and stares at George with astonishment.

"Okay. I'm going to leave you now, I'm tired," Jean-Louis announces. "I've been working a lot lately, I'd better get some sleep if I want to be in shape tomorrow."

It is clear he wants to give them the space they need

to have a private conversation, and everyone plays along. Airy good nights are exchanged before the man disappears into his tent. *What now?* The young woman feels something inside her let go. Could she talk to George about what she's been brooding about for some time already?

"Ekma?"

Monica doesn't answer right away. She stands up to go over to the log where Jean-Louis was sitting a few moments earlier, closer to George. She looks at the fire, its dance foretelling a turbulent time for their day of canoeing tomorrow.

"I noticed it, yes, but I didn't want to accept that it was important. I think it visited me on the beach in Pessamit too. I saw it once when I went walking. And the time after that, it was you I noticed there."

She falls silent, which George welcomes with his own quiet.

"Actually, since last summer, I've been dreaming a lot about a large bird… At first, I didn't pay any attention to it, I didn't realize. And later, I thought…I thought I'd encounter it in the city, but well, anyway…it's as if the raven… I don't know, really, what it means."

She looks at George, who lowers his eyes. Monica can't read his expression. The broad brim of his hat hides his features. He's thinking. After a few seconds of silence, his voice cuts through the air.

"Do you know the thunderbird?"

"The what? No…what is it? Who is it?"

"It's a big bird like an eagle, or a condor, let's say. When the first white people arrived to colonize our lands, we stopped seeing it." George's voice is disarmingly gentle. "If you encounter it, you must be ready."

"Why would I see it? I mean, I've never heard of it before."

George brushes aside her objection. Monica understands: she didn't know its name, but it knew her.

"We are told it is very powerful. It hunted during storms because that's when the little animals come out of their burrows. That's why our ancestors associated it with thunder. In the south, there are legends saying just the opposite. We heard the noise of the storm when it spread its wings. There are a lot of storms around here in July. Less often in October, but it happens when it's due. Monica, I think you have to prepare yourself, that's why you're here."

"Wait… I'll see it for real? You think it'll come back? But…what do we do? How do we prepare for it?"

"What do your dreams say, nituassim?"

Monica feels her heart skip a beat. Nituassim, my child—that's what George just called her.

"I don't know…I'm mixed up. Before, I wasn't sure what beach it was. Now I know it was in Pessamit. Often I'm on that beach, and everything is dark. It's as if my heart is beating in the clouds. That it's going boom in my head. Sometimes I'm afraid, sometimes I'm calm. As if I knew what it was, that it was perhaps even me, the bird…but then I said to myself—"

Suddenly, the rumble of a storm is heard, a dull roar in the distance. Monica jumps to her feet without taking her eyes off the man. "Did you hear that, George?"

"Eshe…"

On the horizon, the dark clouds that have kept growing are rent by a lightning bolt that seems to plunge through the surface of the lake.

"It's far away, it'll go past us. I'm going to bed, my dear."

"Huh? What, already?"

"You'll have to think about the rest of it all on your own. Only you know what the bird has come to tell you." The old man stands, and he walks slowly toward his prospector tent. He barely bends to enter, then disappears inside.

Frightened by the last revelations, Monica prefers to put out the fire, and rushes to her own tent, curling up in her blankets.

Monica knows she's dreaming.

It's the first time this has happened to her, that she is consciously allowing an invisible force to carry her to Ashini Street.

She is walking through the streets of Pessamit. Everywhere, in the alleys that run along the houses, families are busy loading their pickups or the trailers behind their cars.

Everywhere, suitcases, pails of grease, and bags of flour and rice are passed from hand to hand. Tools and utensils stick out haphazardly, along with other accessories necessary for survival. Some people are even trying to load furniture in their trucks.

She stops near a family. The men are carrying a big television set.

"What's going on?" she asks. "Where are you going?"

It's as if no one has heard her question. Everyone continues loading the vehicles without paying any attention to her. Are they abandoning the village? She doesn't see her family anywhere. Where are they? Have they already gone inland too?

She has to find them before they're too far away, before it's impossible to find them. Frantically, she dashes toward the hills on the other side of Route 138, hoping to find them there. Her strides get longer and longer. At the top of the slope of Takutaut Street, she leaps into the air and lands in a place without trees, where electrical pylons dominate the landscape. Their wires crackle with tension, and lights blink weakly. Without hesitating, she crosses the space from west to east. Another stride, and she arrives in the middle of the forest.

Under the cover of the trees, a rumbling shakes the earth. Monica wonders for an instant whether she's the one who caused the tremor, but her doubt fades when a booming cry rings out in the air. She turns around, looking for the source.

A giant she-bear rears up not far away. She is taller than the highest pylons. The bear advances with a slowness that defies the laws of gravity and its effect on her huge mass. Monica doesn't know how to react, whether she should try to run away…or stay. At the last second, trying to jump out of the path of the animal, she manages only a little leap forward, toward the bear, as if the animal's very presence is pinning her to the ground. The earth shakes again, it vibrates.

The big bear, her movement suddenly free of what was impeding her until then, starts running in Monica's direction, each stride accompanied by wails that seem to last an eternity. Monica, filled with panic, abruptly collapses. As the bear charges, it tears out the electrical cables, and they can't hold up the pylon, which also crashes to the ground, producing another shock wave.

When the wave washes over Monica, her fear evaporates. The She-Bear comes up to her, right in front of her. When she touches her, Monica feels that she and the She-Bear are one.

From each direction, each cardinal point, three other gigantic female creatures appear, rising from the horizon.

Monica recognizes to the west the Marten, to the east the Wolf, to the north the Caribou. And she, the Bear, has come from the south to take her place in the Circle.

After a short but gruelling portage, the canoes are put back in the water. It is time to paddle again.

Even though she only had one bag to carry during the march, and she only helped Jean-Louis support the big canoe in the steepest segments, Monica is exhausted. She feels like she didn't sleep the whole night, which stayed stormy until dawn but gave way to a clear morning. Her last dream especially affected her. Her body sends her a thousand signals to remind her that she leaped high and far. She hurts everywhere and her muscles are drained—when she pulls on the paddle beside the canoe, she doesn't feel like she's really propelling the boat forward. They are still two nights away from the destination George planned. No one asks too many questions about the number of kilometres they have to cover on foot or by water, or about the obstacles ahead. George leads the way, and they follow. Monica, who's not used to such an easygoing attitude, tries from time to time to probe him, usually obtaining only half answers. *It's a meaningful place… The men of your family went there… You're not bad at spotting loons, we'll go see if you'll be as good as your great-grandfather at spotting what lives there…* Nothing he says reassures her about the ordeals that await her.

They stop for dinner, pulling the canoes ashore one after the other, with Rich and Annie bringing up the rear.

When the couple gets to the shallow waters close to the bank, the other canoes are already high on the shore, and Monica, with Camil's help, is unloading a few bags containing what they need to cook the meal.

Annie gets out first, stepping out of the bow when it begins to slide up on the sand.

Rich steps into the river, but just as his foot touches the rocky bottom, he collapses in the water, which covers him almost completely. "Aaah! Shit!"

Everyone turns when they hear his scream of pain.

"Rich! What's the matter?" Annie yells, wading out to him.

The others drop what they're doing to run to the shore, Jean-Louis making sure to first tie up the abandoned canoe higher on the sand, while George stands up with difficulty from the stump where he has just barely sat down.

"I think I stepped on something sharp…" Shamefaced, Rich explains that he wasn't wearing his boots, it makes the paddling easier.

"Honestly!" Annie chides him.

"I wasn't careful… It must have been a stone shard." Rich moans with pain, and Jean-Louis and Camil help him up.

"Monica, get the first-aid kit!"

Monica rushes over to the bags and, after searching for a few moments, pulls out the kit and runs back to the men who are helping Rich sit down on the beach, where it's dry.

Annie, amazingly calm, rinses then examines the open wound in the sole of her husband's foot, which is bleeding profusely. The others hold their breath, waiting to know more about the seriousness of the situation.

"Ah! It'll be okay, dear. It's just a scratch, a nasty one though, you know, but it just needs to be cleaned. Then after, you'll have to put on your boots, eh."

The whole group sighs with relief.

Monica kneels on the ground beside Annie and Rich and opens the big red box, which is well-stocked. Up close, she notices that Annie's hands are shaking, but the young woman manages to wrap a long bandage around the injured man's ankle to slow down his circulation and stanch the bleeding.

"It's lucky we have someone who's almost a nurse," Jean-Louis remarks, seeing how confidently Annie treats Rich. "Lucky you were here!"

"It looks worse than it really is. I wouldn't have wanted to see a piece of rock stuck in his foot, for instance..."

The knot of worry in Monica's belly slowly loosens. Yes, it could have been worse. Monica hadn't considered that injuries and accidents could occur on a journey like this, far from any hospital. She promises herself never to forget it. While they're out here, they can count only on themselves to ensure their safety. The understanding hits her and forces a return to reality. Reality...? The young woman feels very far from herself today, with all those dreams that disrupt her sleep and that this new fright has just revived. For an instant she is no longer certain she has witnessed a real event. Assuming it was, was it really chance, or should she see it as a sign? Everything is mixed up.

While Annie tends to the wound, the others busy themselves making dinner, and the joy of being in a place so huge and magnificent slowly restores the atmosphere. Once she has finished preparing the ingredients for the meal, Monica leaves Camil to take care of the cooking, and she goes to sit down with George. During the panic before, he is the only one who really kept his cool.

The Elder looks at her with infinite benevolence, the gaze of a grandfather on his granddaughter.

"You look so much like your grandmother," he whispers.

"It's not the first time you've told me that! I find it funny. I don't have her curly hair...or her dark skin..."

"No, it's the way you act. She was like that when someone needed help. When we went into the woods, she wanted to do everything. I miss her..."

Monica is touched by the sad look that appears on George's face. So, they travelled in the woods together... She tries to imagine all the time spent loving a person, without ever being able to give them that love. And then that person is gone. The love becomes that much more impossible.

"What do we do now that Rich is injured? Will we be able to go on?"

At first, George says nothing, looks around. Annie and Jean-Louis form a chair with their arms to carry Rich to the fire that Camil has finished lighting, sitting him down comfortably so he can elevate his injured foot.

"We'll take a day to rest. It will make the trip longer, but we'll do what we need to do to stay a day more. Gather food around us, hunt small game if we have to. There's partridge around here. With a little luck, we'll be able to catch one or two. Jean-Louis knows how to cook them. It'll make good food, better than the dry stuff we brought."

George stands up slowly. Monica follows him with her eyes. He walks to the forest and enters it without saying another word. Monica stands up, but Jean-Louis comes over to her, a bundle of tent sheeting in his arms.

"He'll be back soon. He does that sometimes. He goes for a walk, especially when he comes to a new place."

"Oh! He's not afraid? He's vulnerable, right…" she says worriedly.

"Monica, an old Innu—even very elderly—is like a young Innu in the woods. There's no stopping George. Come and help me set up his tent instead of staring into space!"

Monica again glances toward the trees where George disappeared, then follows Jean-Louis to give him a hand.

I touch the earth for the first time
in my life.
My hand
grasps the pulsing of cells.
The lichen drinks the sweat of my palm,
all my thirst
for knowledge.

With a start, Monica wakes up from another dream, one even more frightening than the others. She is alone in her tent, and it's unbearable.

She gets up, opens the zippers one after the other, and goes outside. There she finds George sitting by the fire. It must be past midnight. Everyone else went to bed early. As soon as it's dark, they tend to go to sleep. They have to in order to be ready and well rested the next day.

Monica sits down beside George, happy for his reassuring presence. He seems completely awake, though he must have been alone by the fire for hours.

"George, you're not sleeping?"

The man turns to her, eyes shining in the night. "I was thinking about your paternal grandfather...

"Johnny's dad?"

"Yeah. I knew him, that one. He came to visit me this night... Ah, Joseph..."

Monica holds her breath, and George goes on.

"You know, when we were young, we travelled on the land together, with our families. We were distantly related, but still. I would watch him, I thought he was so strong and brave. His father, Samuel, was also a fearless Innu, and his grandfather, your great-great-grandfather Jacques, the same... He knew things...even magical things... He taught me that the land never leaves us alone. We are never alone here, Monica."

The crack of a branch startles her, but she knows there's no point in looking for the source of the noise. Everything is dark around their camp, they can see nothing beyond what the still burning fire illuminates.

She chooses to serenely accept the presence of whatever is out there, close by, even though she can't explain it.

"Yes, that's how it is. They're like that. Hard to explain but easy to understand."

Monica again turns to George, her mouth gaping.

"I feel it too," he says. "Come on, what do you think? I'm not an idiot!"

He chuckles to himself. Monica, who doesn't feel like laughing at the moment, still has to force herself not to smile. George is such a teaser and so genuine, he is irresistible.

Jean-Louis comes out of his tent too. The two of them greet him with their eyes.

"Well, well! You weren't sleeping either?" Monica asks.

"I went to sleep before, but I've been awake for a while. And then, hearing you whispering, I thought I might as well get up too."

The wind ruffles the tops of the trees, producing a relaxing music in the dance of the leaves and the branches. Like a greeting.

"Actually, I need to tell you something. I don't want to stress everyone out, but…"

George and Monica are silent. Jean-Louis wouldn't be referring to something insignificant.

"Just now, I picked up the signal, a bit, with my cellphone, and I saw on Facebook that the weather is starting to get really intense back home. The thunderstorm that came close to us headed that way, then turned into a major storm, with really strong winds, and the waves are starting to get high. Apparently they're starting to reach the buildings below Penshu."

George, taking in the news, looks serious. "That doesn't sound very reassuring. Tomorrow, we'll head back. But we'll take another route. We'll go by a lake that will get us back faster to the river where we parked our pickups."

Monica listens to the announcement with dismay. "What? Why do we have to go back? Don't high tides happen every year?"

"Except it's not normal that the water rises as far as the buildings at the bottom of the village. We have to go back, I have to check what the weather is to know what that means for the community."

"It's true, we've never seen anything like that. Except for maybe one time, a story I heard," Jean-Louis adds, his confidence giving way to an unusual uncertainty that worries Monica more than anything else.

"Yeah, it happens," George answers, half admitting something.

"Something's going on," Monica remarks, "and you can't tell me what it is! That's it, isn't it?"

"We don't know what it is either, nituassim," George answers patiently. "That's why we have to go back."

"It's just…it's there, not here! We can still get back there by the day after tomorrow. Tomorrow, we go on, then we come back the following days. What difference would it make?"

Jean-Louis tries to reason with her. "Monica, if your Elder says to you that tomorrow we go back—"

"Jean-Louis," George interrupts. "It's okay."

"We have to go where you told me we were going to go," Monica continues, a lump in her throat. "That's why I came, it's why I came this far, it's to go see that place! You told me that my father's father had found something where we're going! And besides, you told me it was worthwhile, that—"

"It's true. In any case, your ancestors found that it

was worth the trip."

Jean-Louis looks at George with astonishment. "Wait, you told us that you wanted to go there, but if we're headed for Joseph's mountain, it's not the same."

"Listen, son…I just wanted to see, with the girl—"

"You know we'll never get there! The old Labbé might have gone, sure, but it's because he knew how!"

"It's all very well that you understand each other," Monica interrupts, "but I don't know what we're talking about, and that's just it, I want to go there, I want to see, I want to experience that! We're almost there, let's go! Rich isn't as badly hurt as we thought, we can make it. Why return tomorrow when we're almost there, huh? It's as if the closer we get, the more things happen. Even you, you heard them, the—"

"Monica!" George's voice rings out through the camp. The forest rustles all around, as if small animals fled the surroundings when they heard the old man raise his voice.

"Wow," Jean-Louis sighs.

"What was that?" whispers Monica.

"I told you, we're never alone here," George answers simply, letting a silence hang before continuing. "Tomorrow morning, we'll pack everything up and leave. We'll take the lake route and we'll get back to our pickups quickly. The current will be a little faster, but everything will go well."

George stands up and heads to his tent. Monica and Jean-Louis stay still for a moment without saying anything. Then Jean-Louis starts telling the story of Joseph. He speaks in a way Monica has never heard him speak since the beginning of the journey. Without ever taking his eyes off the embers, Jean-Louis recounts what is said in the village about the time Joseph went all alone to his mountain. There were two companions in the camp, men he often went hunting with. It was a hard year, and the families of Pessamit had given up on going out on the land. But not Joseph. He was in his prime, and he set out alone. And came back with something different in his heart, something he had found there. George was a young man at the time, and people suspected that Joseph had told him what he had seen, on his mountain, but he never opened up about it with anyone else. Jean-Louis heard that story through other village Elders. Without finishing his sentence, he groans, gives himself a shake, and heads back to his tent too, stomping in frustration.

Monica, standing close to the fire, which is dying down as the wood burns up, finds in the darkness a certain sadness. She doesn't understand what has just happened but thinks it would be better to return to the shelter of her own tent. She is suddenly exhausted.

Burrowing into her blankets, she dreads being visited by another incomprehensible dream. How could George go back to bed without batting an eye after what they heard, with the presences that manifested themselves just before Jean-Louis's outburst and his bad news? He went to go back to sleep as if there was nothing, left her with her questions about the stories and the visions around her mushum. It's all very confusing. Now, tomorrow, they have to turn back.

She feels a big knot in her belly. A mixture of anger and, above all, disappointment. She wished those feelings no longer had a hold on her, she would like not to feel so disappointed. But now that she knows, that she really knows she's Innu, and that she knows she has never lost it, that identity, that her feeling of alienation was just another of those damned consequences of the residential schools, of their genocidal schemes, yes, now that she knows, she absolutely has to go all the way. She is sure George was right to want to take her where her grandfather went before her, to find peace, answers, something she senses is essential. Why, why, why turn back now?

All that emerges in that instant, in the storm of her thoughts and her inner turmoil, is tears. A few start to fall, and Monica wipes them away, hoping to erase them, but all the others follow. In her pillow, she tries to stifle her rising sobs. And then, once the rain has passed, she falls into a deep sleep.

The ride down the river, swollen by a torrent a little stronger than expected, grabs Monica's attention and forces her to concentrate, and she forgets what she's been feeling since the day before. When George announced the change of plans in the morning, without providing many details, no one protested. They likely thought it was out of concern for Rich, whose injured foot still couldn't take any weight.

Comfortably settled in the canoe, Jean-Louis's cousin seems to be doing okay, but the way he has to sit to ease the pain in his foot means he can't paddle, his balance is too precarious, so he's sitting in the bow, with Jean-Louis in the stern to both propel and steer the canoe. With Annie behind her, Monica learns the hard way to paddle and steer the canoe through the rapids.

At times, when the others are behind Monica's canoe, she lets a few tears run down her cheeks. Without ever turning around, pretending to be absorbed by what's happening in front of her, watching the current, Monica manages to hide her emotions. Though no doubt George knows, she says to herself. He guesses everything, he sees everything. Her anger at him is fading little by little. Even though they didn't reach the mysterious promised destination. She feels he is acting like a grandfather to her. A strong figure. A mentor.

After a last bend in the river, the group finally reaches the lake that will bring them closer to their starting point. It's a huge lake bordered by hills, much longer than it is wide.

"It will go fast. Since we're going with the current, we'll be able to make quick progress."

As if to prove George wrong, a headwind picks up. Soon it raises waves that pound the bows, sloshing water into the canoes. Monica, seeing the water accumulating in the bottom of her canoe, turns around to make eye contact with Annie.

"It's normal, don't worry," says Annie. "Here's a bailing scoop. When you need to, you bail out the water. But it'll never be enough to sink us, don't worry. Keep paddling."

"But it feels like we're hardly making headway!"

"It's an illusion, Monica. You think that because you're seeing the waves coming toward us, but we're moving forward, and we're still going fast enough."

The wind swells again, hitting them full force. George, trying to keep his hat on his head, looks up to the sky. There are only a few clouds. Yes, it's starting to cloud over, but those clouds aren't bringing the wind. He feels his heart beat a little stronger, worried that he can't read the signs anymore. Can he still guide the group?

From his position in the rear, he is watching, as best he can, the lead canoe. He notices Monica, paddling furiously, determined in her movements, just as valiant as in her inner struggle, in her quest.

The wind grows stronger still and the waves get bigger. Even the current seems to be changing. Before them, through the trees, a cliff appears, forcing the canoes to pivot to the right. Monica is awed by the vertical rock walls stretching toward the sky, unmoving. Almost as if they wanted to become their own horizon.

"Watch out!" Jean-Louis shouts across, his voice carried by the wind. "The wind is pushing us toward the cliff, we have to steer and keep our heading. The current is with us, we just have to be really careful and stay straight."

Monica takes it in and tries not to panic. She wants to turn back to Annie again, search her face for a visual confirmation that everything is going to be okay, but she has to concentrate on what's in front of her. She replays Jean-Louis's advice from that morning over and over again. *Imagine a line in front of you*, he told her before they left, *you'll be leading us. Remember that George is last.*

In a flash, she remembers that strange dream, the one with the flying lungs. She remembers the fluorescent red beams of light that crossed the field and decides that's the line she'll imagine to lead them. A red line, with just enough light to be seen by the others behind. It is enough to believe that it's real.

Her concentration keeps her moving, reaching toward the goal. But just then, a branch blown by the wind brushes against her hair, against the current, flying due north, and she is again overcome by her disappointment of the night before.

Why go back south? What awaits her there? Will she never find that place, which is so hard to reach but where her grandfather managed to go, and where perhaps she too was meant to go? Her frustration at being deprived of that knowledge increases, takes up all the space, weighs down her limbs.

Suddenly, big gusts of wind take her breath away. It's like they're blowing the air straight from her nose to her mouth, depriving her lungs. She is suffocating. Maybe nature itself is angry that these people haven't taken her as far as that meaningful place. But that's absurd: Why would she be the one suffocating? Determined not to show the others that she is struggling for air, she fights on. To breathe. You can't paddle for long without oxygen.

Waves are still smacking the bow of her canoe, spraying her face. It's as if the wind has clamped a watery hand over her mouth and her nose. Monica starts crying, raging against her weakness. The other members of the group are probably going through the same thing, but in her case, the fury of the elements is striking all the accumulated emotion in her belly, her disappointment, her pain. She was making this journey for her grandmother, making this journey for her mother. She was hoping to bury a piece of their past out on the land, somewhere beautiful and infinite, so the three of them could start over. Why did everything have to be so messed up? Now she's suffocating, she's paddling with all her might, she's crying. Between sobs, she is gulping for air.

She squeezes her eyelids shut and tightens her grip on the paddle, paddling, deprived of breath, deprived of light. And then she sees again the Maliotenam residential school, the empty lot, the fence, the blue sky. Her little grandma surrounded by those walls, frightened, separated from her family, and finally emerging from those vile buildings, years later, a young woman, dismal, violated, damaged.

With every fibre of her being, Monica feels the suffering of her past life searching for a way out. An unfamiliar anger swells in her body, until it threatens to tear through her skin. She feels like vomiting. She wants to burn everything, before the little children walk through the residential school doors. But it's impossible, so she paddles, blindly.

In her body, deep down in her body, she sees her mother again, in her solitude, in her pain, in the loss that never seems to end. Deprived of the most important things by a broken mother, she wasn't able to be a mother either when her turn came. But the evil done to her daughter had begun far away, and not deep inside her, any more than within her own mother.

Monica knows that in front of her mirror, every morning, her mother sees her, her daughter, as she herself sees Claire's face. There are mothers and daughters who don't look like each other at all, but Monica is the spitting image of her mother. They mirror each other constantly. Every day of their lives. Monica opens her eyes, turns her face to the sky and stops paddling, lets her weeping occupy the entire space. She is gripped by a strong impulse to throw herself in the water, like a longing to beg the water, the lake, the wind for relief. The cliff, the hill, the trees. The pain is visceral, it cuts through her body and creates a rift in her soul.

She screams.

Monica, rising onto her knees and letting go of her paddle, screams like she has never screamed before.

I certainly have no right to scream my anger at the

spirits. It must be against nature. I don't know. I don't know anything about it.

That regret never stops. Maybe George disapproves, maybe the spirits will disapprove. But why go so far and never reach the destination? Why not be able to finally touch the earth farthest north, if there was any chance of finding peace there? How else can she heal from all the history creeping along the Saint Lawrence?

She screams that wordless need.

Her breath is given back to her through the first scream, and she knows it's to allow her to scream even louder, as loudly as possible. She feels, she knows, she has to dig down deep to let a shriek out, and only through that cry will she be able to tear away the veil that separates her from the unseen.

I don't understand your visions. I don't understand what you want with me. I've been alone my whole life. I've cried my whole life. I've carried the pain of being denied my own existence my whole life.

They convinced me that I shouldn't have existed, that I shouldn't have lived. That my presence in the world was a burden. One element too many. They deliberately hid my history from me and they separated me from my identity. I didn't even know that Innu *means human being! Human beings, dehumanized, lived through the very worst things possible.*

Who are you? What are you doing, so far inland, hiding from my gaze? I know you're here, I was coming to you, and you're sending me away. I want you to see me, to hear me! Or else I'll make sure I haul you out of your sleep.

I was told that the energy of the land is impossible to call up, to tame, that we can't make it bend to our will, but today I'm lost and I'm calling you.

Take my suffering! I don't want it anymore.
Take my pain! I don't want it anymore.
Give me back my breath. I am not alone.

Monica screams. A last cry floats away on the wind. She opens her eyes.

Around her, everything changes shape, perspective. The elements calm down. They're past the cliff. But she no longer knows where she is.

Red veins, almost transparent, run through the air, the water. On the shore, the trees are dancing, little shadows passing furtively between their trunks. A big brown being, walking like a human, crosses a clearing, farther on, on the shore.

She has the impression that everything is breathing with her. Each second, the beating of a heart runs through everything, uniting everything. The whole universe is connected.

Suddenly, she sees George, who silently signals to Annie and to Monica to head toward the shore close by. The others have already headed in that direction. Monica can't hear anything but understands that he wants to let most of the bad weather go by. Her vision is no longer so vivid, and she tries to retain what remains of it. Her canoe comes up on dry land, but she doesn't sit down right away with the others. She walks away from them and comes to a little stream beside which she feels the touch of a familiar presence.

Perhaps I can finally see it. After all this time.

She walks into the water without realizing it. Her eyes fill with tears again. She comes to a rock in the middle of the stream, higher than the others, and sits her tired body down for a moment. She is still shuddering with weeping, and soon the presence becomes stronger, enough to make her look up. "Who's there? I want to know!"

Something is right in front of her, farther away in the stream, still hidden by a few bushes.

She recognizes a red checked shirt. Black pants, held up by braces. She recognizes the broad shoulders, she's seen them in photos. Mushum Joseph. At that precise instant, standing in front of her. Present. The image is blurred by the salty water in her red eyes, but she can make out his features as a young man, as powerful again as he was in the prime of his life. Is it true, when the Innuat die, that their spirits return to the land? Do they become young again?

A vision. She sees many Innuat, dressed according to different eras, going back out onto the land. She sees them, farther along, taking their places. She can't keep from blinking her eyes a few times, to try to wipe away the tears, but instead of shedding light on her waking dream, the movements erase her mushum, and everything she perceived so clearly an instant before—the breath, the connection—starts to slowly evaporate.

"No!" she whispers.

She closes her eyes, lowering her head, her body slumped against the rock. She waited for the return of the weight crushing her breath, but instead a lightness sweeps through her body, starting from her belly.

She opens her eyes and notes with a pang that she can again see as she did before. But everything has changed. The world is absolutely calm. Nothing moves anymore, the wind has dropped.

She hears someone approaching and tries to stand up, but she slips and has to lean against the rock still warm from her body, from her tears.

"Monica?"

George is walking toward her, emerging from a thicket she passed through to get to the stream. The water has returned to a peaceful song, and its surface shimmers. George is standing in front of her, very straight, a slight smile on his lips.

"Are you ready?"

The question, spoken in the heat of the sun that is now shining strongly through the cover of the trees, is loaded with every meaning possible. For Monica, it resonates, it is the most important question, the one to which she wants to give the most important answer.

"Eshe."

George lays a confident hand on her shoulder, and the two walk together that way toward the others, who are sitting a little farther away.

"When we come back, nituassim, we'll speak Innu, okay?"

"Okay, mushum."

I have come from so far.
To put my foot on the rock. The river is my cradle.
My spirit is at peace now. Nothing more can make me
doubt who I am.
My grandmother can close her eyes.
My mother can sleep.
I have swallowed the storm.

I have become the Sky.

Silence.

Darkness.

Marie-Anne, what's happening to me?

Your heart opens up when you come back here, to your home. All your cells recognize the river of your people. And when you go back into Nutshimit, the territory remembers our footsteps. It remembers our daily strides, our perilous portages, the language of our ancestors.

When Innuat return to the land, the cycle of life can start again. It stopped beating when they created the reserves and built the dams. Even if we forget, the land never forgets us. It will always wait for our return. It dreams of again feeling the softness of our footsteps on its velvet skin, hearing us laugh and sing the old songs again. The same songs it gave us.

When you come back home, yes, it will be like the salmon against the current. But your memory will give you back the strength to return to the land where your spirit was born. Where all our ancestors await us. To help us heal. To help us understand. To help us come back to ourselves.

What is happening to you is merely the visible and the invisible finding each other through you. You're the passageway of our reconnection. You and your generation will give us back the memory and the path to Nutshimit.

Cosmos.

There is panic in the village. Everyone is gathered on Laletaut Street, the water lapping at their ankles. It's unimaginable. Some of the houses on Metsheteu Street are already flooded. Families are loading bags and suitcases into their cars. First the Elders are evacuated, even if it's only to take them to higher ground, outside the village. After that, some are talking about a place where many have cottages. Yes, that's a good way to keep everyone safe. They're trying to load as many people as possible into each vehicle. There'll be time to come back later for supplies, for whatever things can be saved.

The storm is raging.

Monica was able to get Laurie on the phone. The whole little family is safe in the house, which is far from the shore, and there is no fear that the water could come that far. Their main concern is the wind, which is blowing strongly enough to send debris flying through the air. Outdoor furniture crashing into windows, breaking them. But it will be okay. Laurie, her sons, and Marie-Anne are sheltering in the basement. They just have to wait out the storm. Reassured, Monica leaves George's house and runs to Laletaut Street.

When she gets within sight of the river, the scene looks like many of the dreams she has had. She recognizes everything. A storm is gathering offshore, and there are sinister black clouds covering the whole village. Children are crying, women are yelling.

In spite of the powerful winds, a worried crowd has gathered by the shore. The people in the group seem to have given up on building barricades and are totally involved in observing something in the sky. Monica, who rushed down, can't see what everyone is looking at, even though she tries to follow the direction of their eyes.

In a great crash of lightning, the Thunderbird appears.

She recognizes it.

It gives a shrill cry, splitting the air with bolt after bolt of lightning, and a huge growl of thunder shakes the world.

People start screaming, fleeing, and trying to get back to the shelter of the very houses they evacuated a short time before. One fear displaces another.

The gusts gather strength again. With each flap of its wings, the Thunderbird creates a vibration like an earthquake.

Monica is alone, facing the breakers. A gust of wind almost knocks her over and she notices, farther back, a few individuals half-sheltered by cars and sheds, watching, dumbstruck, while others can't keep themselves from staring at the fiery creature. Monica turns her dark eyes back to it.

It's not a raven.

It's not a dream.

Thunderbird, protector of the forests, the game, and the people, I know who you are.

The great bird of my nights is you.

The stars fall, breaking through the heavy clouds, and tumble toward the waves. A prayer rises in Monica, and

right away she speaks loud and clear to Nanimissu-Metshu.
In Innu-aimun. Her language.
A chant.
Everything slows down.

Take us back to the land
Take us back to the forests of yesteryear
Restore the forests, restore the cliffs
Take us back to our ancestors
Take us back to Papakassik"
Take us back to the caribou
Free us
Free us from history
Free us from despair
Free us from the wound that tore us from our territory
Free us from the yoke
That erases our languages, our beliefs
Free us from power games
Free us
Free us from the pain of the residential schools
Free the children buried under the sand
Free the bodies lost in the woods
Free us
Free our bodies
Free our spirits
From alienation, from scorn
Soothe the spirit of our parents
Of our grandparents
Of the ancestors
Soothe the spirit of our children
Soothe us
Give them the fire
That will carry them all the way

Give them the strength
To reconnect their people
With memory
May your presence
Bring us the power
To change
The course of history
To restore
The cycle of the seasons
May your cry
Bring us out of famine
And lead us to abundance.

Lightning.

This is the path. To stand in the middle of the trees, each of them ten times taller than we are. To stand up without doubts, without being afraid to be silent, to listen to the voice of the shadows.

To stand up.

And believe in the ancestors.

Ninashkumuau my father, Jean-Pierre. Suzanna, Andrew, for your patience. For your unflagging friendship: Marie-Kristine, Maïlys, Catherine, Karen, Gabrielle, Jemmy, Alexandre, Jay, Randy. Sabryna, my best friend always, always there for me, always there at the right time. Myriam, you are extraordinary for your patience, your listening, your generosity. Sayaka, for your words. Joséphine, you and me forever. Through poetry, you brought me back home, to Pessamit. Tshinashkumitinau nutam etashiek. <3 The Conseil des arts et des lettres du Québec for funding this project. It meant a lot to me. Tshinashkumitinau.

This book is a love letter to survivors of residential schools. You survived, you gave us life, and now we are here. We brave all the storms you could or couldn't get through. You survived because your strength is enormous. We have taken up the torch, and even though sometimes it seems to go out, it is never dead. Nothing and no one has ever been able to put it out. I hope through this book to feed that inner fire.

I dedicate this book to the descendants of residential school survivors. To overcome the history imprinted in our bones is an enormous task. It is a daily challenge. With this book, I want to contribute to us finding our way, finding our voice again, beyond the traumas that have often prevented us from moving forward, from being ourselves, from being wholly ourselves. We are overcoming the imposed suffering, we are overcoming all the storms. We walk the streets and we again speak our languages. We are again singing our songs. We are again learning our legends and we are reclaiming the sovereignty of our narrative. This era is ours.

NOTE: In keeping with the wishes of the author, the spellings for Nations and communities named in this book are those usually favoured by the groups in question; likewise for derived adjectives (for example, the nouns *Innu* and *Innuat*, and the adjective *Innu*).

NATASHA KANAPÉ FONTAINE is an Innu writer, poet, and interdisciplinary artist from Pessamit, on the Nitassinan (North Shore, Québec). She lives in Tio'tia:ke, known as Montreal. Her critically acclaimed poetry and essays are widely taught and have been translated into several languages. In 2017, she received the Rights and Freedoms Award for her poetry and her contribution to bringing people closer through art, writing, performance, dialogue, respect, and cultural exchange. In 2021, she received the Chevalier de l'Ordre des arts et des lettres de la République française. She also works as a translator, screenwriter, sensitivity reader, and consultant on Indigenous literature.

PHOTO: JULIEN LAJOIE-LEMAY

HOWARD SCOTT is a literary translator living in Montreal who translates fiction, poetry, and non-fiction, often with Phyllis Aronoff. He received the Governor General's Literary Award for Translation for *The Euguelion* by Louky Bersianik and, with Phyllis Aronoff, won the Quebec Writers' Federation Translation Award for *The Great Peace of Montreal of 1701* by Gilles Havard. The translating duo were also awarded a Governor General's Literary Award for their translation of *Descent into Night* by Edem Awumey. Scott is past president of the Literary Translators' Association of Canada.

PHOTO: JACQUES PHARAND

Colophon

Manufactured as the first English edition of
Nauetakuan, a silence for a noise
in the summer of 2024 by Book*hug Press

Edited for the press by Katia Grubisic
Copy-edited by Stuart Ross
Proofread by Laurie Siblock
Type + design by Malcolm Sutton

Printed in Canada

bookhugpress.ca